I0669341

They rape me with smiles on their faces - but I will deal with them seriously.

A LADY WHO TARGETS MARRIED CELEBRITIES TO REVENGE RAPE

Robert Adehin

 New Generation **Publishing**

ACKNOWLEDGEMENTS

First of all, I thank God, father of all, who gave me the wisdom, knowledge, understanding and strength to complete this book. I would like to express my heartfelt thanks to my beloved late father High Chief Isaiah Ilemobayo Adehin, and my mother Most Rev. Mother Folannah DIdunyemi Adehin, for their blessing.

No one walks alone on the journey of life. I would like to use this opportunity to thank Mojoyin Akinde, Oriola Adehin and his family, Bolanle Eniobama, Remilekun Akinde, and my children: Funmilayo Adehin, Temitayo Adehin, Eniola Adehin and David Adehin, for their endurance, understanding and encouragement.

Words are inadequate for offering my thanks to Rev. L.O Farojoye, Rev. J.O Farojoye (USA), Pa Omowanle, Dr. N. Gadong, Chief O. Ofoesuwa and his family, Benson Fadaini (Solicitor) and his family, Boboye Fadaini (Lawyer) and his family, T. Okunlowo (Solicitor), D. Bolarinwa (Barrister), Felix O. Akinsete and his family, Snr Rev. Mother C. Farojoye, Commander S. Alagba, Snr Rev. Mother Towolawi, Eucharia C. Denis Onyenanu, Comfort Olorunsuyi and her family, Betsy Strasser, Mike Ingington, Rev. O. Legbe and the entire members of the C&S Church of Zion (Imole), Rev. R. Mafolabomi and the entire members of the C&S Church of Zion (Walthamstow), Rev A. Akintimehin and the entire members of the C&S Church of Zion (North London), Rev. Teokumu and the entire members of the C&S Church of Zion (Bermondsey), Rev. S. Towolawi and the entire members of the C&S Church of Zion (Odo Ayo), for their spiritual support, advice and moral support.

Finally, my thanks and appreciation goes to my workmate Henrietta Obilana, Pooney Sekar, Sandra

Brighton, Lesley Caller, Gloria Onwubiko, Ade Adetoro, Vida Asiedu, Lesley Roast, Christine Palmer, Wendy Hawkins, Jacqui Brewster, Folake Richardson, Sandra Munonye Gift Osafo, Claire Huolder, Lesley Huolder, Michelle Duffy, Matt Price, Abidemi Olateju, Adebola Dehinbo, Mary Pierre-Marquis, Leon Maxine, Laurence Maxine, Pragna Patel, David Chinnery, Rumena Begum, Sharon Brown, Renee Bruce-Annan, Joanne Grant, Sinead McManamy, Binu George, Rachel Thomas, Fatma Maawiy, Aysha Begum, to mention a few, for their support and encouragement.

May our Lord meet you in the point of your need in Jesus' name (Amen).

It may sound funny that Kate targets the married celebrities for her revenge instead of reporting the boys that raped her to the authorities for them to be dealt with.

Kate was a close friend to Paulina and they were both born in the countryside by middle family.

Paulina became Kate's friend when her family bought a house near Kate's family. Although they were both born in the countryside, their villages were different.

Kate's father was a farmer while her mother was a housewife, helping her husband when necessary. But Paulina's mother owned a grocery shop, managing it with the help of her daughter while Paulina's father worked in the call-centre as a manager. Kate and Paulina went to the same primary school. Sometimes Paulina's mother would take Kate and Paulina to school and also collect them. If Paulina's mother was occupied, Kate's mother or father would take them.. This routine made the two families very close to each other.

The family of Kate and Paulina became so close that they ate dinner together several times. When Paulina was six years old, her mother became pregnant with their second baby. Grace, Paulina's mother, kept this to herself because she wasn't sure about the pregnancy. After three months, Grace went to Lucy, Kate's mother, to tell her the news of the pregnancy.

One day on Friday evening, when Paulina's mother Grace closed her shop, she went home to prepare dinner for her family . After dinner, she went to Kate's mother Lucy's house and knocked at the door. Paulina's father opened the door and Lucy asked: "Can I come in?"

"Yes of course," Stephen, Paulina's father, replied. As Grace was about to enter, Lucy came out from the kitchen.

"Are you alright Grace?" Lucy asked..

"I'm fine, thank you," Grace replied. "I have come to see you."

Lucy said, "Come, let us go to the living room."

Lucy faced her husband and said in a funny voice, "Could you please excuse us for a moment – it is women's talk." She was joking with her husband. Stephen smiled and looked at Lucy's face while Grace covered her mouth with her right hand so as not to burst into laughter. Lucy held Grace's hand and said, "Lets go." She then looked at her husband with a sideways look and signed to him with one eye.

Lucy and Grace went to the living room and Lucy asked, "Are you alright?"

Grace replied, "Yes, I'm fine. I have news for you, although I should have told my husband before I came to you. But I'm not certain about it yet."

"Are you pregnant?" Lucy asked, with smile on her face.

Grace looked at Lucy's face as she was about to break the news. Kate called her mother as she was walking down the stairs. Lucy answered her, but Kate didn't hear her mother's voice and continued shouting, "Mother – mother, where are you?" Lucy came out from the living room and said, "Here I am."

"Can I go and play with my friend Paulina?" Her mother looked at her face without saying anything. Kate continued by saying, "Please, please, mum." Lucy used her head to show Kate that she should enter the living room.

Kate entered the living room and saw Paulina's mother. "How are you, Kate?" Grace asked.

"I'm fine, thank you," Kate replied. "Where is Paulina?"

"She is at home," Grace replied.

Kate faced her mother again and said, "Please – please, mother."

Lucy looked at her face and said, "Go."

"Thank you, mum," Kate said as she was running towards the door. "Dad I will see you later," Kate said as she opened the door. Then Dad came out from the toilet, and said, "Where are you going?" Kate was already out, and he closed the door. She couldn't hear her father's question. Stephen went to the living room to ask Kate's mother where Kate was going.

"She is going to play with her friend Paulina," Lucy replied. Stephen then went back to the room to relax .

"Now Grace, tell me that you are pregnant," Lucy said.

Grace replied, "Yes! yes!"

They both held each other's hands and continued to jump and shout with happiness.

Stephen wasn't sure what was going on; he could hear Grace and Lucy shouting, and he came down to see what was happening. As he opened the living room door, he saw Lucy and Grace holding each other's hands and jumping for joy. When Lucy and Grace saw him they stopped; Lucy signed to her husband with one eye and said, "We will see you later." When Stephen saw that there was nothing happening to them, he went back to his room.

In the living room, Lucy and Grace then sat down after their jubilation.

"Now tell me how it's happened," Lucy said.

Grace replied, "It's the work of God."

"Do you think it was a miracle?" Lucy said.

"Yes, it's a miracle from God not from a human being at all," Grace replied.

"What do you mean; it is from God not from human being?"

"I have been trying several times for a baby and I

have used many things but nothing seemed to happen."

"Do you mean you have tried all the expertise and doctors?" Lucy asked.

"Yes my friend," Grace replied. "Look at Paulina's age; she is six years this year. If I did not have any problems I could have had two babies by now, but because I have a problem, it's not possible. I even tried IVF twice but all failed. That is the reason why I do not want to tell my husband yet." As Grace was talking, tears started to drop from Lucy's eyes.

Grace held her hands and asked,, "Did I say something that annoyed you?"

"No," Lucy replied. Grace gave her a tissue to wipe her eyes. Lucy looked at Grace and they held each other's hands and burst into laughter. Then Lucy said, "Likewise, I have been trying for many years now – but all failed. I and my husband had given up because of the doctor's advice. Sometime the experts get it wrong."

"You can see my own example now," Grace said.

"Your own example is one out of hundreds," Lucy replied. "I know that the doctors and the experts are always getting it right."

"But as it's happened to me, it can also happen to you,", Grace said.

"Amen," Lucy replied. "Let me prepare you tea. "

"That would be very nice," Grace replied.

"Do you want sugar in your tea?"

"Two sugars please," Grace replied.

Lucy went to the kitchen to bring cups of tea for herself and Grace. "How are you going to break the news to your husband?" she asked.

"I don't know," Grace replied.

"I think Joshua will be pleased when he hears the news," Lucy said.

"I don't know how he's going to react to it, simply

because both of us had given up really! Lucy, you know this is not an easy matter."

"What do you mean by that?" Lucy replied.

"We have got used to a certain routine in our life that needs to be changed. I do not think that it will be very easy to change" Grace said.

"Do you mean that you have got used to the idea of running your business and Joshua is concentrating on his job?" Lucy asked.

"Yes, exactly," Grace replied. Lucy laughed.

"What are you laughing at?" Grace said, as Lucy continued giggling. Grace relaxed on the sofa while Lucy finished her giggling. When Lucy stopped giggling, Grace asked, "Could you tell me the reason why you are giggling?" Do you realise that many people are looking for this blessing?"

With a smile, Lucy replied, "The only thing I can say to you at this moment is that the baby is more precious than your business.

Grace looked at Lucy's eyes with a smile, shaking her head with a funny voice. "I know I know. With a lower voice Lucy said, "You need to tell your husband about the baby and hear his opinion."

"I know that he may give up his job to look after me and the baby."

Lucy looked at Grace's eyes with a smile and said, "What are you looking for again?"

Grace smiled with a funny voice and replied, "I am looking forward to getting this little precious thing out of my stomach."

They both burst out laughing. "I am always here for you," Lucy said. Grace looked at her eyes with a smile and shook her head ups and down, with the words in her mouth: "I know I know." They cuddled each other and sat down to enjoy their tea. Not more than two minutes later someone knocked at the door. Lucy stood up to go and open it. It was Grace's husband Joshua.

"Hi Lucy," Joshua said.

"I'm fine, thank you; "Lucy replied in a funny voice. "I think you are looking for your wife?"

"No, I already know that she's here," Joshua replied.

Thinking that Joshua had come for her, Grace stood up to tell her husband that they should go. But Joshua said, "Relax yourself, I came to see Stephen."

"Kate, go and call your dad in the bedroom," Lucy said.

Kate held Paulina's hand and said, "Let us go together." Paulina and Kate ran upstairs, and while Kate was shouting, "Dad, Dad, Paulina's father wants you." Stephen came out from the bedroom to meet Kate and Paulina on the stair landing. Kate held her dad's hand walking down the stairs while Paulina followed them.

Stephen entered the living room with Kate and Paulina.

"Hi, how are you Steve?" Joshua asked.

"I'm fine, thank you," Stephen replied.

"What are you doing this weekend?" Joshua asked.

"We do not have any particular thing we are doing," Steve replied.

"Could we visit the beach tomorrow to enjoy the beautiful summer?" Joshua said. Before Joshua finished his statement Kate and Paulina jumped up and said, "That would be great".

"But I'm opening my business tomorrow," Grace intervened.

"Do not worry about tomorrow, God will provide," Joshua replied.

"That would be better," Stephen said.

"Are we going with two cars?" Joshua asked.

"No, we can go with my Jeep," Steve replied.

"Lucy and Grace, are you alright with the idea?" Joshua said.

"That's brilliant," Lucy replied with a deep funny voice.

"Now what can I offer you Joshua?" Lucy said.

"A cup of coffee with one sugar will be great," Joshua replied.

"What about you Stephen?" Lucy said.

"A cup of coffee with two sugars please", Stephen replied. Lucy went to the kitchen to put on the kettle. A minute later Grace followed her. "Do you want to break the news to your husband now because he seems to be very happy today?"

Grace said, "No, no, this is not the right time."

"Are you going to call him in the middle of the night and tell him?" Lucy asked

"If he is angry because I woke him up in the middle of the night, what can I do?" Grace said.

"Why is he going to be angry?" Lucy asked.

"He loves to sleep and he doesn't want anybody to disturb him when he is sleeping," Grace said.

"Even though he's angry, when you tell him the news he will forgive you," Lucy replied.

"Okay, okay! I will do that," Grace said.

Lucy and Grace left the kitchen with the cups of coffee they had prepared for Stephen and Joshua. In the living room, Grace gave a cup of coffee to Joshua, while Lucy gave Stephen his own cup of coffee.

"Thank you very much," Joshua and Stephen said to Lucy and Grace.

"With my pleasure," Lucy replied.

"We are all going to enjoy ourselves tomorrow at the beach," Stephen said.

"Yes Dad," Kate replied without allowing anybody to talk before her. They all looked at Kate's eyes. Then Grace said, "Kate, why are you and Paulina are so excited by tomorrow's outing?"

"We have been waiting for this moment so long," Paulina replied.

"What do you mean by that?" Grace asked. Paulina moved towards her mother and placed her left hand on her right shoulder. She looked at her mother eyes and said, "Mum how long has it been since you and Dad took me out me out?" Grace looked at her father's eyes and looked at Paulina's face with a sideways look and replied:

"But your father took you and Kate to your friend's party last week."

Paulina left her mother and moved towards her father and said, "Dad, I'm not talking about a party here, now I'm talking about visiting a park, leisure centre, circus etc."

Stephen, Lucy and Grace focused their attention on Paulina as she was talking.

"But before we moved here, we normally took you to the park, circus movies etc.," Joshua said. Paulina turned away from her dad and stood in front of her mother, and looked at her face.

"Answer your father," Grace said.

Paulina moved to her seat and as she was about to sit down, she said, "Mother how long have we been in this village?"

Grace looked at her husband's eyes and kept silent. The living room was quiet for some moments. Stephen broke the silence by saying, "From today on we, your parents, will be taking you and Kate out all the time."

"Thank you Steve," Paulina replied.

Joshua looked at Grace's eyes and said, "It getting dark, let us go home". He stood up and held Paulina's hand.

"Bye, bye, Paulina, see you tomorrow," Kate said.

Joshua, Grace and Pauline let themselves out. As

they were walking to their home, Grace said, "Your father and I were very sorry for not taking you out. But you could have called us at home and told us instead of you telling us out."

Joshua opened the door. They both went in. "Do you hear what I said to you, Paulina?" Grace asked..

"Mum, you and dad are so concerned about business and jobs; you don't even have time for me anymore."

"That is not true," Joshua said.

Paulina left them and ran to her bedroom upstairs and shut the door. Grace wanted to go after her and bring her down to the living room but Joshua said "Leave her alone, she's upset."

Grace and Joshua entered their living room and sat down close to each other. Joshua put his hand round Grace's neck and said, "What can we do now? Let us leave her alone to cool down then we will talk to her".

After thirty minutes Joshua went upstairs and knocked Paulina's door. "Come in," Paulina said.

Joshua opened the door gently while Paulina was in the bed, facing the wall. Joshua said, "We are very sorry about what happened."

"That's alright Dad," Paulina replied, turning her face to Joshua. Joshua kissed her forehead and said:

"I will see you tomorrow."

Paulina smiled and said, "I love you, Dad."

"I love you too," Joshua replied and shut the door.

On the following day after breakfast, Joshua called Stephen to be prepared. Stephen's family and Joshua's family went to the beach to enjoy themselves. On the beach, Kate and Paulina were happy, and were running around the beach. Stephen, Joshua, Lucy and Grace sat under the tent watching Kate and Paulina.

"Do you think we have enough time for these kids?" Stephen asked.

"What do you mean by enough time? We take them

to the school activities and parties sometimes," Grace replied.

"Yesterday I could see that something was bothering them," Stephen said.

"What do you think we can do?" Joshua asked.

Lucy intervened. "We need to call them and ask them what is on their mind."

"You are right," Grace replied.

Joshua went out of the tent and called Kate and Paulina to come in. Kate and Paulina's bodies were full of beach sand.

"Are we going home, Dad?" Paulina asked.

"No, we just want to talk to you and Kate," Lucy intervened.

"About what?" Kate said.

Lucy moved towards Paulina and Kate and held their hand; she bent down and said, "We just want to know what is bothering the two of you."

"What do you mean, Mum?" Kate replied.

Joshua, Stephen and Grace were looking at Paulina and Kate's faces to know their reaction. Lucy paused for some seconds. "We could see how Paulina talked to her mother yesterday and we are thinking something is bothering you." Paulina looked at her mother's face and said, "I'm sorry, Mum." Grace cuddled her and said, "That's alright."

"Now tell us what is bothering you and Kate", Lucy said.

"We just want you to have more time for us," Kate replied.

"What do you mean by time, Kate?" Joshua asked.

"We just want you to take us to the park, beach, family show, funfairs, where all of us could come together as families," Kate replied.

"Is that us?" Stephen said.

"Yes," Kate and Paulina replied by shaking their

heads up and down.

"We promise you that from today on, we will have time for you," Stephen said.

"Thank you Dad and Mum," Paulina and Kate said and ran out from the tent to the beach. Grace came out and looked at them as they were running round the beach and playing with sand. She could see that Paulina and Kate were very, very happy

"I could see that they were so happy," Grace said.

"Why not, when both of us do not have time for them?" Joshua asked.

"Where is the time?" Stephen said, "When I am busy with my farm and Lucy my wife is busy with domestic work and sometimes helps me out when it's too much for me. While Joshua is going to his work from morning to evening every day and Grace his wife will be busy with her small business."

"Please, we do not need to feel guilt. The only solution to this problem is to discuss how we are going to spend some time with them," Joshua said

"What do you reckon, Stephen?" Lucy replied.

"Every Saturday we need to share it among us to take them to where they want to go" Stephen said.

"That will be very difficult for me, simply because I'm open on Saturday," Grace said.

Joshua intervened. "Do not think there will be a problem at all, because any time you are not available I will go with them. If I could not go with them, you could sacrifice one day not to open your shop."

"That's alright," Grace replied.

"Are we all agreed?" Lucy said in a funny voice.

"Yes we are," Stephen and Joshua said and laughed.

Joshua brought a bottle of wine out and poured it onto four glasses and gave it to Stephen, Lucy and Grace. But Grace refused to drink her wine; she said to Joshua, "I prefer orange juice." Joshua poured orange juice in another glass for Grace. They were all drinking and chatting. After ten minutes Grace excused Lucy outside the tent and they both walked along the beach. "Do you think this is a perfect time to tell my husband that I'm pregnant?" Grace asked.

"Yes, it will be perfect if the two of you are walking along the beach before you reveal it to him," Lucy replied.

"Thank you, my friend." Grace cuddled Lucy and they both went to the tent.

"Where have you been?" Joshua said to Lucy and Grace.

"We went for a women's mission," Lucy replied with body language and funny voice. They all laughed because Lucy was funny.

"You cannot win them," Stephen said.

"That is very sure, because we are mothers," Grace replied.

They all sat down in the tent and chatted for about half an hour. Grace said to Joshua, "Please could you excuse me for some seconds?"

"Woman again." Joshua replied with a deep voice.

"Yes we are," Lucy intervened with a funny voice. They all laughed; Grace held Joshua's hand and they went out of the tent. Joshua wasn't aware what Grace was going to say to him. He thought that probably Grace wanted to discuss her business or how she was going to create more time to pay attention to their daughter.. That's what was in the mind of Joshua.

As they were walking along the beach Grace said "Joshua, I have surprise news to tell you."

Joshua, in a funny manner, ran into the sea with his trousers wet and threw some sand in the air and replied, "I cannot wait to hear the news, love."

Grace, with a smile on her face, said, "You haven't heard the news yet, Joshua."

"I know my love, I'm just excited about your news whether bad or good, we can both deal with it," Joshua replied.

"Thank you for your sense of humour," Grace said.

As Joshua was about to say something, Kate and Paulina ran along the beach splashing water on both Joshua and Grace . Joshua ran and followed them into the sea and splashed water on Paulina, Kate and Grace. Paulina and Kate retaliated by splashing the water into Joshua's face. Grace stood by the seashore, laughing and watching them. Paulina and Kate left Joshua and ran to Grace at the seashore, holding her hands, and dragged her into the water. Grace splashed water on Kate and Paulina, while Joshua, Kate and Paulina also splashed the water into Grace's face. After some time, Grace and Joshua faced each other with the water splashing in each other's faces. Joshua carried Grace in his arms and looked with emotional love at her face and said, "I love you, dear." Grace gave Joshua kisses by circling her hands round his neck, and replied, "I love you too." By this time Kate and Paulina had left Grace and Joshua in the water, running around the beach.

Grace still circled her hands round Joshua's neck and Joshua carried her. Grace said, "Dear, I have good news to tell you."

"I cannot wait to hear the good news," Joshua replied.

"I'm pregnant," Grace said.

"No, no," Joshua replied, in a loud, happy voice.

"Yes, yes," Grace said.

Joshua kissed Grace several times and said repeatedly, "I love you, I love you."

"Love you too," Grace replied. Joshua threw Grace into the water, and they both splashed water on each other's faces with happiness and joy.

Lucy came out of the tent and looked round the

beach to see Grace and Joshua because she knew what Grace was going to say to Joshua. Lucy could see Grace and Joshua and how they were splashing water in each other's faces and kissing each other. She was very happy for Grace. Lucy back to the tent without saying anything to her husband.

After the romantic and emotional feeling between Joshua and Grace, they went back to the tent to break the news to Stephen and Lucy. When Joshua and Grace walked in, Lucy could see a big smile on Grace's face. But Lucy pretended that she didn't know what was going on.

"Stephen and Lucy, we have good news to tell," Joshua said.

"Have you won a lottery?" Stephen replied in a funny and deep voice.

Joshua smiled and said, "This is more than winning a lottery, friend." Stephen paid attention to what Joshua was going to say. With anxiety, Joshua declared the news that: "My wife is pregnant; we are going to have a baby". Joshua kissed his wife and cuddled her with the words, "I love you, dear."

"I love you too." Grace replied.

"Congratulations." Stephen shook Joshua's hand and hugged Grace.

"I'm very happy for you, Joshua," Lucy said.

"Thank you very, very much," Joshua replied.

Joshua's family and Stephen's family enjoyed themselves on the beach that day. They later returned home in the evening when the sun went down and it was very dark on the beach. Joshua and Grace didn't break the pregnancy news to their daughter Paulina until they reached home. Paulina was so delighted that she was going to have a brother.

Then Stephen and Joshua's families shared their available time to take Kate and Paulina to where they liked to go in their leisure time. Kate and Paulina were so happy that their parents devoted their available time to them.

As time went by, Grace was so heavy in her stomach. To run her business day to day became a problem. Grace discussed this matter with her husband and they came up with the solution that Grace needed to employ somebody to look after the shop; instead of her closing it down during her pregnancy. Joshua and Grace advertised in the local newspaper. Many turned up for the interview, but eventually they gave the job to a local lady called Margaret. Margaret's house was not far from Grace's house. This gave Grace easy access to co-ordinate her business very well with the help of Margaret. Joshua was really pleased for Grace that she had found a local lady that was trustworthy to run her business for her. Margaret was happy to get something to do locally.

One day Lucy went to collect Kate and Paulina from school. On their way back they stopped at Grace's shop to say hello to Margaret and see how she was coping. Fortunately, Grace was in the shop with Margaret. Immediately Paulina and Kate entered the shop, Paulina said to Margaret, "Could I have one chocolate please?" Margaret signalled to Paulina that her mother was at the back of the shop. Paulina ran to her mother at the back of the shop and said, "Mum, could Kate and I have one chocolate please?"

"Yes, you can," Grace replied. Paulina took chocolate and asked Kate what she was going to take.

"I will take the same as yours," Kate replied.

As Kate and Paulina were eating their chocolate, Margaret asked them, "What do you plan to be in the future?" Kate looked at Paulina's face and smiled. Then Margaret said, "I'm talking to you, young ladies."

"We plan to be teachers in the future," Kate replied.

"What about you, Paulina?" Margaret asked.

"Kate has answered your question, Margaret," Paulina replied in a polite manner.

"We discuss what we are going to become in the future any time we are playing in the school play ground," Kate said.

Lucy intervened. "Do you mean you and Paulina?"

"Yes Mum," Kate replied. By this time Grace had come out to join them in the front shop. Lucy looked at Grace's face and Grace intervened. "They are clever kids; they know what they want to be in the future."

"How could you know at your early age that you are going to be teachers?" Lucy asked.

Paulina moved towards her mother and held her hand and said, "Look at my face Mum." Grace looked at her face and paid attention to her. "Anything we want to be in the future as a friend is for you to support us as a parent. Remember the decision has to be taken by us not by our parent."

Grace kissed Paulina's forehead and replied, "Love, I'm not the one who asked you the question. The question was asked by Kate's mum."

Paulina left her mother and put her hand across Kate's shoulder and turned to Kate's mum and asked, "Are you going to support our decision?"

Lucy looked at their faces and replied "Yes love," by nodding her head."

"Do you promise, Mum?" Kate asked.

"Yes, I promise," Lucy replied.

"What about you, Mum?" Paulina asked.

"Yes, I promise," Grace replied.

"Let us go home in order for you to have rest," Lucy said.

"Yes, Mum," Kate replied. Paulina and Kate entered the car and Lucy drove them home to have a rest.

Kate and Paulina finished their primary school and

entered the same secondary school. They kept their promise to become teachers by reminding each other at all times. They also worked hard to obtain good grades in their advanced levels in the same subjects. After their advanced levels they both gained admission into the same university in the capital. Kate and Paulina were motivated by the help they received from their university for their ambition to become teachers to be fulfilled. They could have gone to university closer, but Kate made the suggestion that they should go far from their families to enjoy another life. Maybe because she was a sociable and outgoing person, while Paulina was a little bit reserved. Kate and Paulina's families were delighted that both of them gained admission to the same university. The family thought that they would look after each other as they had done from primary school to secondary school.

Kate and Paulina lived in the same dormitory in their university and they were both doing well. Kate was a sociable person who quickly got on with the male classmates. But Paulina felt reluctant to associate herself with male classmates simply because she thought that they would look at her as a cheap woman.

One day in the classroom, after a lesson, Paulina was talking to Kate about the lesson they had just finished. Kate's man friend Rufus intervened to talk to Kate. Paulina looked at his face and said, "Please could you let us finish our discussion before you intervene?"

"I am not talking to you, I'm talking to Kate if you don't mind," replied Rufus.

"But you know that we were talking before you intervened," said Paulina.

"That's your problem," Rufus replied.

Paulina was about to talk, Kate intervened. "Stop arguing, the two of you."

Paulina was so angry and left them.

"Do you know that, you need not to be rude Rufus?" Kate said.

"I'm sorry to embarrass you Kate," Rufus replied.

"Now I'm listening to you," Kate said.

"What are you doing tomorrow night?" Rufus asked.

"Is there anything special?"

"Not at all, we were going to a night club tomorrow, would you like to go?" Rufus replied.

"I don't know yet, I need to talk to Paulina first, okay?"

As Kate was about to go Rufus called her and said, "I will pay for the expenses if you don't mind."

"Thanks Rufus, I will talk to you later," Kate replied.

Kate went to the dormitory to meet Paulina to apologise for what had happened. Kate knocked on Paulina's door.

"Who is it?" Paulina asked.

"It's me," Kate replied.

"Go away, I don't need your problems at this moment," Paulina said.

"Please open the door, I come to apologise."

Paulina opened the door and blocked the entrance. "What can I do for you?" She looked at Kate's face with dazzling eyes.

"Please can I come in?" Kate asked. Paulina moved out of the way for Kate to come in. "I come to apologise for what happened today" Kate said.

"That is what you like, to associate yourself with all these rough boys," replied Paulina.

"I do not come here to argue, I come here to apologise, right," Kate said.

"Your apology is accepted, go your way," Paulina replied with anger.

"Why do you have to be harsh with me, Paulina?"

Kate asked.

"I'm not; I don't want anybody to treat me as a stupid person."

"Is it me or who's treating you like stupid?"

"You and your friend," Paulina replied.

Kate stood up and moving round the room, said in a funny voice, "Is it today I will begin to treat you as a stupid person?" She paused and laughed.

"After all, we grew up together; we went to the same primary school, the same college and have the same ideology, also our families are great friends since they have known each other.. Today we are in the same university and the same classroom doing the same course and because of a man friend I will throw all these away and be treating you badly. What type of person do you think I am?" Tears dropped from Kate's eyes.

Paulina was so moved she stood up and tapped Kate's shoulder at the back and said, "I'm sorry. I'm sorry too."

They both laughed and found something to eat. As they were eating, Kate said "What are you doing tomorrow night, Paulina?"

"Is there any big thing happening tomorrow night?" she replied.

"Not really, Rufus just wants to take us to a club, if you don't mind?" Kate said.

"Do you mean the guy that was talking to you in the classroom?"

"Yes!"

"I'm afraid I cannot go and waste my time hanging around with that type of guy in a club," said Paulina.

"We are not going with the guy alone, there are some other guys that going with us," Kate replied.

"Who's going to pay the bills?" she asked.

"The guys will pay the bills," Kate replied.

"Can you count on them?" Paulina asked.

Kate went to her room and phoned Rufus and told him that Paulina was going with them, if he didn't mind. "Yes, that will be great", Rufus replied.

Kate relaxed for a couple of hours and in the evening she went to the university library to do some reading. Kate was about to come home when she met Rufus in the library entrance with some guys.

"Hi Kate, are you alright?"

"I'm fine, thank you," Kate replied. "Are you still on for tomorrow night ?" Rufus asked.

"Yes, of course" she replied.

Rufus then introduced the boys to Kate. "Hi guys" she said.

"Are you coming with your friend tomorrow?" Ian, one of the guys, asked Kate.

"Yes, I'm coming with my friend Paulina," she replied.

"Is she beautiful like you?" Ian said. He was joking.

"Of course, she's prettier than I am." Kate tapped Ian's jaw and left.

"That is cool," Ian said, looking at Kate back as she was going. Ian looked at Rufus's eyes with a sideways look.

"Don't even try it" Rufus said.

"Why should I resist a beautiful woman like this?" Ian replied.

Rufus turned to Ian face to face and said, "She's my friend; you should treat her with respect because she is a respectable lady."

"Yes, it's alright." Ian put his two hands up. They both went to the library for their studies.

After finishing in the library, Ian came to Rufus to apologise his behaviour. "Rufus, I didn't mean to upset you earlier on," he said.

"I have already told you that anybody I'm dealing

with I want you and the other guys to treat them nicely," Rufus replied.

"I know but sometimes you get carried away by something or other, which happens to everybody, including you," Ian said.

"What do you mean? Are you telling me that you got carried away with Kate's beauty?" They both laughed.

"No, I'm not talking about Kate, I'm talking about what happens to every human being, sometime, in every aspect of life," said Ian.

"Your apology is accepted, please don't do it another time."

"Yes, mate." They both shook hands.

As they were walking toward the dormitory - "Ian, do you know that your words remind me that I should apologise to Kate's friend Paulina also?" Rufus said.

"What happened between you and Paulina?" Ian asked.

"She intervened when I was talking to Kate after the lesson today and she wasn't happy the way I talked to her."

"If you know that you are guilty in your mind then go and apologise to her." Ian said.

"But it is too late to go to their dormitory tonight, I will do that tomorrow morning," Rufus replied.

"Do as it pleases your mind, friend," he said.

"Maybe you should remind me tomorrow if I forget," Rufus said in a funny and deep voice. They both laughed and went to their dormitory.

In the morning after breakfast they went to the ladies dormitory to knock at Paulina's door. Paulina was still in bed. She opened the door and saw Rufus; she was so annoyed she banged the door in his face. But Rufus continued to knock and said, "Please Paulina, open the door I have come to apologise."

Paulina replied, "Go away, I do not know you".

He continued to knock. Paulina called Kate, who was still in bed, on her mobile phone that Rufus was at her door and that she should come and get him away. Kate came in pyjamas and saw Rufus knocking Paulina's door.

"What's your problem Rufus?" Kate asked.

"I've come to apologise for what I did to her yesterday," he replied. Kate was so pleased with Rufus's reply and his attitude, that she knocked at the door and Paulina opened it "Please could you take your friend away?" Paulina said with anger.

"What is your problem, he has come to apologise for what he has done to you," Kate replied in a polite manner. Paulina went back to bed and Kate and Rufus entered the room. Paulina covered her head with bed sheet; Kate sat on the bed while Rufus sat on the only chair that was available. After two to three minutes Kate said, "Please, Paulina, could you give us some respect by uncovering your head and listening to what we're going to say."

Paulina removed the bed sheet from her head and sat down with Kate on the bed.

"I know that this a bit of an awful time for you. I myself wasn't happy when you called me because I was still in bed. But for someone to realise that he has done something wrong when nobody forced him to come and apologise for what he has done, we should give him credit and treat him in a polite manner," Kate said.

"Please, I'm really sorry about that," Paulina replied.

Rufus smiled because he was so impressed with the way Kate made Paulina apologise. Rufus opened his mouth, "Paulina sorry to come and knock your door at this awful time. Since yesterday I have felt guilty about the way I talked to you after the lesson, that's why I come to apologise, if you can forgive me."

Paulina looked at Kate's face with a smile and cuddled her and started to cry.

"I'm sorry, I'm sorry" she said.

Kate tapped her back. "Don't cry, I'm with you always."

Rufus was moved by Paulina and Kate's friendship and was speechless. After Paulina regained herself, she wiped her tears with her pyjamas, stood up to move towards Rufus, shook his hand and said, "I have forgiven you". Rufus thanked Kate for her effort to resolve the problem, and promised to see them in the evening. Rufus left the room and Paulina thanked her friend Kate. Kate also thanked Paulina for accepting Rufus's apology. They prepared breakfast and ate together.

On his way to the dormitory Rufus started to think about Kate and Paulina's relationship and promised himself to go out with one of them.

Rufus went to Ian's room to tell him that he had apologised to Paulina. "How did she react when you apologised to her?" Ian asked.

"I had a rough time when I first knocked on her door," Rufus replied.

"Tell me about it," Ian said, with anxiety to hear the bad news from Rufus.

"She opened the door and when she saw me she slammed the door in my face."

"Oh, that's a disgrace to your integrity," Ian said, squeezing his eyes in a funny way.

Rufus continued. "I knocked again and again. She shouted inside her room without opening the door: 'Go away, I don't know you'."

"I would have walked away if it was me," Ian said.

Rufus laughed at Ian's statement. "What are you laughing at, Rufus?" Ian asked.

"If you walk away that means you are not going there to apologise," Rufus replied.

"Do you think everybody can have that type of patience?" Ian asked.

"Why do you go there to apologise then?" he replied. "Anyway when I continued to knock she didn't open the door but two minutes later I saw Kate come in her pyjamas. She said 'What do you think you are doing Rufus?' I replied, 'I've come to apologise for what I did to Paulina in the class after the lesson yesterday'."

"She might have called Kate on her mobile phone," said Ian.

"I think so," Rufus replied.

"What happened after that?" Ian asked.

"Kate knocked the door and she opened the door."

"Kate is your saviour, you could have been in a mess," Ian said in a funny voice.

"Yes", Rufus smiled and continued. "We both entered Paulina's room; she covered her head with kit in the bed."

Ian intervened "That was to show you that you're not welcome."

"You are right, but what amazed me was the way Kate changed her mind to listen and accept my apology, it was unbelievable."

"You are lucky that Kate is around to solve the grievances between you and Paulina," said Ian.

"I'm damn lucky," replied Rufus with a smile.

In the afternoon Rufus and Ian went to the shopping centre to do a little bit of shopping. On their way, Rufus said to Ian, "I was impressed with Kate and Paulina's attitude today and I have it in mind to go out with one of them."

Ian laughed. "Do you mean a relationship?"

Rufus paused for some seconds. "Yes."

Ian looked at Rufus in a funny way and started laughing.

"Could you please tell me the reasons for you to be laughing, Ian?"

"After all that you went through this morning you're still attracted to these people?"

"I wish you were there this morning to see how Kate handled the matter," he said.

"Is that the only reason for you to be attracted to them?" replied Ian.

"That is enough for me," Rufus said.

"Which one do you prefer then?" asked Ian.

"I haven't made up my mind yet," he replied.

"Lucky you, friend, but be careful. Remember yesterday you told me not to try at all, that they are your friends or have you changed your mind?" Ian said.

Rufus looked at Ian's face with a smile and replied, "Your no today'', ''Maybe your yes tomorrow.''.

"Which means I could go for either one of them," said Ian. Rufus laughed and Ian was expecting him to say something. But Rufus continued laughing.

"Say something, friend," Ian said. Rufus looked at Ian's eyes as he was laughing and tapped his shoulder and said, "You also want a good fish."

"What do you mean by a good fish?" Ian asked with a harsh voice.

"I mean a good lady," Rufus replied.

"Yes I do," he said.

"Beware of fire my friend because you may get burnt."

"I'm a grown up person you know."

"I know, but fire has no respect of anybody," Rufus replied.

In the evening after Rufus and Ian had had enough rest, they prepared for their night out. They went to the school campus where their friends Martin and Johnson are waiting for them. The guys chatted for some minutes, and Rufus decided to call Kate on her mobile phone.

"Hi Kate," he said.

"I'm fine," Kate replied on the phone. The guys were joking with Rufus that he was calling his girlfriend, not knowing he was calling Kate. "I could hear some talking in the background. Where are you calling from?" Kate asked.

"Yes, my friends are joking with me that I am calling my girlfriend," Rufus replied.

"Are we all going together?" she asked.

"Yes, if you don't mind," Rufus replied.

"No, that will be great fun," she said.

"We are in the school campus waiting for you and Paulina."

"We are on our way, see you later," she replied.

Kate and Paulina wore their best clothes for the outing, simply because it was the first outing since they had been admitted to the university. Rufus and his friends saw Kate and Paulina in their outing dresses and they were amazed. Immediately Rufus fell in love with Paulina. They all picked up a cab and went to the night club.

In the night club Kate quickly adapted herself to the guys by dancing and drinking with them. But Paulina remained reserved by drinking orange juice with Rufus who didn't touch alcohol.

"Rufus, why did you not take alcohol like the rest of your friends?" Paulina asked.

"I would have liked to but I cannot," he replied.

"Why?" Paulina asked.

Rufus could not hear her properly because of the music. They moved to a quieter place. "Why don't you taste alcohol?" Paulina asked again. As Rufus went to open his mouth, tears dropped from his eyes.

"I'm very sorry to upset you," said Paulina.

"That's alright," he replied. Paulina gave Rufus a tissue to clean his eyes.

"Thank you very much," Rufus said.

"Have your drink," said Paulina.

Rufus poured his drink into his mouth and looked at Paulina's face with a smile and said, "I'm alright now."

Paulina replied, "That is better," with a smile on her face.

"You're a great lady, you know. I am very sorry to talk to you rudely on that day," he said.

"That is alright," Paulina replied.

"When I was a child my mother was addicted to alcohol." He paused for some seconds and looked at Paulina's face and Paulina replied with a smile. He then continued, "She was a good mother to her children."

"How many of you?" Paulina intervened.

Rufus looked at Paulina's face, smiling, and said "We're two, my sister and I. I was thinking my father would leave us due to my mother's alcoholic addiction, but I was wrong. She shouted at my father, abused my father physically in our presence."

"Did your father retaliate to the abuse?" Paulina asked.

"Poor Dad would take us and drive to the nearest restaurant for her to calm down."

Paulina shook her head and said, "He must have gone through hell."

"He did," Rufus replied. "He later died when I was eleven years old and my sister was nine ."

"I'm very sorry." Paulina used her hand to rub Rufus's hand.

Rufus replied with a smile and said, "Thank you for listening to me."

"That is alright. Let us go and enjoy ourselves like the others." Paulina held Rufus's hands and dragged him to the dance floor, where Kate and the rest of the guys were enjoying themselves. When Kate saw Paulina and Rufus dancing together she left the rest of the boys and joined them. She danced with them for some minutes and returned to the guys. Paulina could see that Kate was really enjoying herself.

After an hour Rufus and Paulina went back to their seat where they sat down . They told each other about their life stories and what they were going to do after graduation. Rufus asked Paulina whether she would go with him for dinner at another time.

"Is that a date?" Paulina replied with a funny voice. Rufus looked at Paulina, smiling, and said, "Yes, if you don't mind." Paulina, with a smile, looked at Rufus's face with a sideways look and placed her hand on Rufus and said, "You're on."

"Thank you very much," he said and kissed Paulina's hand.

It was five minutes past four in the morning. Paulina looked at her watch and said, "Let me go and call Kate, it is time for us to go home."

"Do you want me to go with you?" Rufus asked.

"No, wait here. I will be back shortly." replied Paulina.

Paulina went to Kate but Kate was so drunk she didn't want to go at that time. Kate told Paulina to give her another thirty minutes. Ian, Johnson and Martin were laughing at her. She pulled Kate by her hand and said, "Let us go home." Kate was so drunk that she did not know what she was doing. She pulled her hand from Paulina aggressively and said, "Do not touch me again, leave me alone to enjoy myself." Nobody paid attention to them, except Ian, Johnson and Martin because the music was too loud. Paulina pulled Kate's hand again, facing her face to face and said, "You're drunk and the guys are making gestures at you. Let us go home."

Kate was so angry she slapped Paulina on her face. "Leave me alone," she said. Immediately Rufus rushed to the scene and took Paulina away. Paulina was humiliated and started crying. Rufus tried to comfort Paulina. After Paulina regained herself he asked her to excuse him for a moment. He went to Ian, Johnson and Martin to tell them it was time for them to go home. When Kate saw that the guys had followed Rufus, she followed them too. They all went out of the club, and Rufus called a mini cab to take them home. After Ian, Martin and Johnson were dropped at the men's campus, Rufus followed Paulina and Kate to make sure they reached home safely. Immediately they got out of the minicab, Kate started to be sick. Paulina and Rufus managed to get her to her room and lay her on her bed.

"Are you going to leave her?" Rufus asked Paulina.

"No, I will stay with her," replied Paulina.

"Where are you going to sleep?" Rufus asked.

"I will sleep on the floor," she replied.

"Do you want me to stay with you?"

"No, I will be alright" Paulina replied

"Do you want tea of coffee?" Paulina asked.

"Where are you going to get that because this is not your room?" Rufus asked.

"She's my sister I know where she keeps her things."

"What do you mean she is your sister? I thought you were just a close friend." Paulina put her hand on her forehead and laughed.

"What are you laughing at Paulina? Am I making a fool of myself?" Rufus asked. He stood up, wanting to leave because Paulina was laughing at him. Paulina held him and gave him a kiss on his cheek and said, "Sit down; I'm not laughing at you."

Rufus sat down and listened to what Paulina had to

say. Paulina looked at Rufus's eyes with a smile and paused.

"Say something," Rufus said.

"You know when I said that Kate was my sister you were a little bit confused.

"Yes. I am," Rufus replied.

"We've known each other since we were about three years old, since then we have been together. Her family and my family share everything together. We went to the same primary school, the same secondary school and now we are in the same university doing the same course. Not only that we have the same ambition to become teachers in the future. That is the reason why I said she's my sister. Do you still want your tea?" she asked.

"With two sugars please," Rufus replied. Paulina prepared a cup of tea for Rufus and coffee for herself. As they were drinking the tea and coffee Paulina thanked Rufus for his help.

"That is alright" Rufus replied. After Rufus had finished his tea he said, "It is now time for me to go and have a little rest." He opened the door and Paulina kissed him to say goodbye. Rufus was pleased with Paulina's kiss and the way she treated him.

After Rufus left Paulina, she slept on the floor to relax herself and also to monitor Kate and see that she was alright. Kate was so drunk that she did not even remember what was happening around her. About 3 o'clock in the afternoon Kate woke up and saw Paulina on the floor sleeping. She was so terribly ashamed of herself for what she had put Paulina through.

"How did I get home, Paulina?" she asked.

"I could have been in a mess if Rufus hadn't helped out," Paulina replied.

"Do you mean Rufus helped you to put me in bed?" she asked.

"Yes," Paulina replied.

"What about the rest of the guys?"

"After the mini cab dropped us they went to their dormitory, but Rufus stayed to help me out," Paulina replied.

"Was I in a terrible state?" Kate asked.

"You were," Paulina replied, "You were even sick when we are trying to help you home."

"Did I mess myself in the presence of Rufus?" she asked.

"And so, you just drunk as much as anybody else," Paulina replied. "Now let me go to my room to have rest," Paulina said.

"Could I prepare something for us to eat?" Kate replied.

"No, let me go and have my shower first then I will come back," Paulina replied.

After her shower, Paulina decided to have a little rest before going to Kate. She switched off her mobile and lay on her bed. After Kate had finished preparing lunch she rang Paulina's phone to tell her that lunch was ready. But Paulina's phone was off. Kate was very angry that Paulina had deliberately switched off her phone to avoid her. Kate waited for another thirty minutes and called Paulina's mobile again. No response, Paulina was fast asleep. She went to Paulina's room, banging the door. Paulina woke up, surprised, and opened the door and saw Kate with furious eyes.

"What is your problem?" Paulina asked.

"I have no problem," she replied "It's you who has a problem," Kate said.

"Why are you continuously banging the door, if you have no problem?" she asked.

"Are you trying to avoid me?" Kate asked.

"No, I just fell asleep, when I wanted to rest my

back for a little bit before coming to you," Paulina replied.

"Why did you switch off your mobile phone?" Kate asked.

"Are you accusing me of deliberately switching off my mobile phone because of you?" Paulina asked. "However, you do deserve it after all that you did to me in the club last night."

"What have I done to you? Are you telling me that it is payback time?" Kate replied with an angry voice and moved closer to Paulina.

"Do you want to hit me?" she said, with anger.

Kate looked at Paulina's face and said, "I don't need to hit you." She paused, "Because it isn't worth it."

"What are you going to do then?" Paulina asked.

Kate opened the door and slammed it with anger. Paulina followed her and said, "What are you going to do now?" She repeated the same sentence over and over as she was following Kate. Kate kept silent and continued walking to her room with annoyance. Luckily for Kate and Paulina, there was no other roommate around during the drama. When Kate entered her room she opened the door and wanted to slam the door in Paulina's face. But Paulina pushed the door and forced herself to enter Kate's room. Kate was annoyed and turned back to her and said, "What is your problem?"

"I have no problem. It's you that has a big problem," Paulina replied.

"Leave my room then," said Kate with a harsh voice. Paulina moved closer to Kate and looked at her face and said, "Hit me, hit me."

Kate looked at her face, shook her head and burst into laughter and said "You bloody bastard, sit down let us have our lunch". Paulina joined Kate in laughing for about three minutes. After they had both cooled down they sat down to eat their lunch.

"Did I mess myself up in the club last night?" asked Kate.

"No," Paulina replied with a funny voice. Kate burst into laughter.

"Why are you laughing, Kate?" Paulina asked.

"The way you said 'No,' I quickly recognise that something happened last night," Kate said.

"What do you think happened?" replied Paulina.

Kate looked at Paulina's eyes, smiling, and said "I know that I made a mess of myself."

"Yes, you made a mess of yourself by giving me a dirty slap when I was trying to get you home," Paulina said.

"Do you mean I slapped you last night?" she asked.

"Yes, you did," Paulina replied. Kate stopped eating and paid attention to what Paulina was saying. Paulina looked at her eyes and said, "Please eat something to regain your strength." Kate looked at Paulina's face, smiling, and said, "I'm sorry that I slapped you last night in the club."

"Not me alone you need to apologise to," Paulina replied.

"Who also do I need to apologise to?" Kate asked.

"You need to apologise to Rufus because were you nearly sick on his legs last night," replied Paulina.

"I will do that if I see him" she said.

"You'd better do that quickly," Paulina replied with a funny voice. After they had finished their lunch, Paulina went to her room to have a rest. Kate also stayed indoors to have a little bit of rest to recover from her hangover from the club.

On Monday Paulina and Kate prepared for their lesson, and they met Ian on the way.

"How are you doing Kate?" he asked.

"I'm fine, thank you" Kate replied.

"And you, Paulina?"

"I'm also fine, thank you," Paulina replied.

"Where is Rufus?" Kate asked.

"He went to the library early this morning to renew his due book," Ian replied.

"I will see him in the classroom. But if I do not see him tell him that I want to speak to him," Kate said.

Ian went to the library to deliver Kate's message to Rufus. "Did she say anything to you?" Rufus asked.

"No, she said, 'tell Rufus that I want to speak to him'," Ian replied.

"Anyway I will see her in the classroom later," Rufus said.

After the lesson Kate and Paulina went to Rufus together.

"Kate, how are you doing?"

"I'm fine thank you," she replied. "Rufus, I want to apologise for my misbehaviour on Saturday night ," Kate said.

"That is alright," Rufus replied.

"Also, thank you for the help you gave Paulina in order to get me home safely," she said with a funny voice.

Rufus looked at Paulina's eyes, smiling, and replied, "You need to be thanking your friend because she did the hard work. I only gave her help."

"I have already thanked her. She's my best friend and I love her from our youth to this present moment and my love will not change whatever she does to me," Kate said, looking at Paulina's face. Paulina smiled and cuddled her. They left Rufus to go to their dormitory. On the way Paulina said, "You'd better stay away from alcohol, to avoid you having to apologise every second."

"Do you mean I should not enjoy myself?" Kate

asked.

"Is it alcohol alone you need to enjoy yourself?" Paulina asked.

"What do you mean by that?" she asked.

"You could enjoy yourself with sex," Paulina replied with a funny voice. They both laughed.

"Do you think I need sex now with all this course work piling up ?" Kate asked..

"It will even make you understand your course work more," replied Paulina with a funny voice and laughter.

"What about you, Paulina, do you need it?" Kate asked with laughter.

"Yes I do," Paulina replied.

Kate burst into laughter and said, "Do you have eyes for anyone among the boys?"

"I have given Rufus kisses to thank him for escorting me and you home safely from the club." Kate looked at Paulina's eyes as she was talking and coughed. "Why do you cough?" Paulina asked.

"This means you have carried on an operation behind my back," said Kate.

"What do you mean by operation?" Paulina replied.

"I know that there is nothing serious going on between you and Rufus yet. But you took advantage of me being drunk to get into his mind," Kate said.

"No, it just happened in the club that we have something in common," replied Paulina.

"How do you know that you have something in common?" Kate asked.

"When we were in the club I noticed that he wasn't taking alcohol like the rest of the guys do."

Kate intervened "Do you mean you fell in love with him before we got to the club?"

"Not at all," replied Paulina.

"Why are you watching all that he is doing?" she said.

"Remember that we had a quarrel on the first day I knew him, and there was no way I could set eyes on him," replied Paulina.

"How did you manage then, did you have a chance to get closer to him?" Kate asked.

"It started when the other guys and you had a little bit of alcohol and were dancing. He wasn't drinking alcohol; he was drinking orange juice and standing in the corner. Then I went to him and asked him why he wasn't drinking alcohol. He told me about his life history and the reasons for him not drinking alcohol."

Kate intervened. "Which means all these sorts of things were going on in the club and I did not know about it?"

Paulina smiled and replied, "Because you were drunk and enjoying yourself with the other guys, it was difficult for me to tell you at that moment."

"Are you telling me I was too drunk to listen to your comments?" asked Kate.

"I'm sorry, you were," Paulina replied. They both laughed for about two minutes. By this time they were about to enter the library.

"We will continue our discussion after we finish in the library," Kate said.

"What are we discussing again? I have already told you what I need to tell you," Paulina replied.

"No, Paulina you need to tell me how far you have gone with him," Kate said.

Paulina looked at her face, smiling, and said, "Alright when we finish in the library."

They both entered the library to do some reading. Throughout the time in the library, Kate kept this thought in her mind, simply because she wanted to know how far Paulina had gone with Rufus. She managed to finish her assignment, but the matter was still occupying her mind.

After they finished in the library, Kate decided to take Paulina to a nearby restaurant for a meal. Paulina realised what Kate was doing to extract information from her about her relationship with Rufus. "Kate, are you taking me to the restaurant to get more information about what is going on between me and Rufus?" she asked.

"No, I just want us to have something to eat," Kate replied.

"Do you think I am a baby?" Paulina said.

"No," she smiled, "I just want to know how far you have gone with the guy. This is the guy you do not agree with, from the day you met him. Also the day he went to apologise to you, you refused to open your door. Suddenly after a night out in the club you become attracted to him."

"Is there anything bad in that?" Paulina asked.

"Not at all, but you need to be careful," Kate replied.

"Okay, I understand. Do you still want to take me to the restaurant?" Paulina said.

"I do," Kate replied. As they were in the restaurant eating, Paulina's mobile phone rang. She checked the number that was on her screen and saw that it was Rufus's number. She signed to Kate that Rufus was the one calling. Kate replied, with body language, that she should answer the call. Paulina picked up the phone to answer Rufus.

"Where are you?" he asked.

"I am with my sister," she replied.

"Do you mean Kate?" he asked.

"Yes," she replied. "Do you want to come and meet us?"

"Yes, I would love to," he replied.

"We are in the restaurant opposite the library if you want to come," she said.

"I will see you in a couple of minutes," he replied.

When Paulina finished the conversation with Rufus she looked at Kate's eyes and smiled. "Now I can see that you're serious about what you're saying about Rufus," Kate said.

"Yes, I am," Paulina replied.

About ten minutes later, Rufus met Paulina and Kate in the restaurant. With a smile on his face he asked "How are you doing Kate?"

Kate looked at Paulina's eyes with a smile and Paulina signed with a sideways look for Kate to say hello to Rufus. Then Kate replied, "I'm fine, thank you."

"What about you, Paulina?"

"I am also fine thank you," Paulina replied. Kate continued smiling and looking at Paulina's face.

"Please have a seat ," Paulina said.

"Thank you" he replied, sitting down near Kate. Paulina knew the reason why Kate was smiling but Rufus didn't know anything. "What are you going to have Rufus?" Paulina asked.

"I would like to have hot chocolate because it's chilly outside there." Paulina was about to stand up to order Rufus hot chocolate. Rufus said, "I will go by myself, thank you". Immediately Rufus stood up to order chocolate, and he asked Kate and Paulina, "Do you need anything?"

"No, we are alright." they replied. Kate looked at Paulina's face and smiled.

"What are you smiling at?" Paulina asked Kate in a funny, deep voice.

"Nothing, my dear," Kate replied in a funny voice.

"I can see that everything is in place for you and this guy," said Kate. Paulina looked at Kate's eyes, smiling, and replied, "I hope so."

Rufus came with his hot chocolate and sat down

with Paulina and Kate. "Would you like to eat anything at all?" Kate asked, smiling.

"No, I'm alright," Rufus replied.

"Where is your friend Ian?" Kate asked.

"He went out with Johnson and Martin," he replied. Paulina looked at Kate's eyes with a smile as she asked about Ian.

"Why did you look at me like that?" Kate asked.

"Is there anything going on between you and Ian?" Paulina asked in a funny way. Kate burst into laughter and Paulina joined in her laughter. Rufus was silent because he couldn't figure out what was going on. After they stopped laughing, Kate said, "I didn't know that you have gone so far with my sister to this extent." Paulina kept watching Rufus to see how he would reply to Kate's comment. Rufus looked at Kate's face, smiling, and said, "Did she tell you anything?"

"No, but I wasn't born yesterday," Kate said. Paulina smiled and kept silent.

"She is my sister, anything she tells me about you is truth, which means you are going for it," Kate said in a funny way.

Rufus looked at Paulina's face with a smile and Paulina replied with a happy smile. Kate pretended that she didn't see them. Rufus replied, "She is your sister; if you could allow me to go for her I would be delighted, with joy in my heart."

Kate lifted her two hands up and said in a funny way, "She is yours, I am not going to allow anything to double cross your way."

"Thank you very much," Rufus replied with a big smile on his face. Paulina also watched Rufus's reaction with a smile on her face. Paulina paused for some seconds with her face down. She lifted her eyes up and looked at Kate's eyes and said, "Are you sure about this?"

Kate looked at Rufus's eyes with a sideways look and looked at Paulina's face and replied, "If that is what you want, I support you with all my heart."

Paulina cuddled her and said, "Thank you very much." Paulina's emotion was so high that she started to shed tears. Kate cuddled her and tapped her back, "Do not cry," she said. Rufus was emotionally moved when he saw Paulina shedding tears. He also cuddled her and said, "Do not cry, everything will be alright."

After they finished in the restaurant, Paulina and Kate went to their dormitory while Rufus went to look for Ian in the university compound. From that day, Rufus and Paulina entered a strong relationship. They began to see each other on a regular basis.

After a month, Ian saw that the relationship between Paulina and Rufus was serious. He decided to go out with Kate. On Saturday afternoon, on a summer day when the temperature was about twenty five degrees Celsius, Rufus and Ian ware cooling themselves with a soft drink in Ian's room.

Ian said, "Please, Rufus, I don't want it to be a surprise to you. I have decided to try Kate, whether something will work out between me and her." Rufus burst into laughter.

"Why are you laughing?" Ian asked."I know that you have warned me not to try either of them. But things are different now because you are going out with Paulina and she loves you. Why can't I try to see I could succeed?"

Rufus looked at Ian's eyes and burst into laughter again. Ian was upset, and moved round the room with his soft drink in his hand.

He said, "I don't see reasons for you to make a fool of me. Do you think you know how to treat a woman more than I do? If you think like that, you are joking".

As Rufus listened to what Ian was saying, he

continued laughing. Ian saw that Rufus wasn't listening to him, and he asked him, with anger, to leave his room. But Rufus continued to laugh, pretending that he hadn't heard what Ian had said. Ian grabbed Rufus's shirt with anger and said, "Leave my room before I call the police for you."

Rufus, with anger, pushed Ian away and said, "You bastard, do you think I don't know your history with women? How you use them and dump them?

"Can't you realise that Kate is a close friend to Paulina and she deserves respect? Or do you want to use her and dump her as you dump the other women? If I see you near her you will be dead." Rufus banged Ian's door and went away. Ian opened the door and said with a loud voice, "Do not come back again, you bastard." Rufus went to his room, while Ian was upset with Rufus's behaviour.

Immediately Rufus entered his room, his mobile phone rang. He looked at his mobile screen and saw that the number did not appear. As he picked up the phone, he heard a voice saying, "Hello, it is me, Paulina."

"Why do you withhold your number?" Rufus asked in a harsh voice.

In a polite manner, Paulina replied, "Why do you have to talk to me like that?"

Rufus realised immediately what he had done and said, "I'm very sorry, dear, I just had a rough time with Ian."

"But Ian is your best friend, why do you have to have a bad time with him?" Paulina replied.

"I will tell you later if I see you," Rufus said.

"Are you free tonight?" Paulina asked.

"What is happening tonight?" Rufus replied.

"Maybe we can go for dinner in a very quiet restaurant?" she said.

"You are on," Rufus replied.

"See you later," she said.

"Bye bye," he replied.

In the evening Rufus met Paulina in a seated place. Meanwhile Ian was terrified about Rufus's behaviour. He thought about what to do next to make up with Rufus. With fear in his mind, Ian called Kate on her mobile phone. "What can I do for you?" Kate asked.

"I wonder if you are not busy tonight whether I could see you because I need to talk to you."

"Is it a date?" Kate replied in a funny voice.

"Anything you call it, it is okay for me," said Ian. Ian was delighted that Kate accepted his offer, However, there was fear in his mind that Kate might come with Paulina which could change his plan, because he didn't realise that Paulina had gone out with Rufus. But when Paulina was going out she rang Kate to tell her that she was going out with her boyfriend. Immediately Kate finished the conversation with Ian, she called Paulina to tell her that Ian had asked her out. Paulina was delighted to hear that she had a date because she didn't want Kate to be bored at home alone when she was going out with her boyfriend. After Kate had finished talking with Paulina, Paulina excused Rufus and said, "That was Kate talking to me on the phone."

"Is she alright?" Rufus asked.

"Yes, she is okay, she says she's going out tonight with Ian."

Rufus reacted angrily by saying abusive words.

"Why do you react like that?" Paulina asked.

"I'm very sorry," replied Rufus. "I was trying to protect Kate from that bastard boy."

"Why do you need to protect Kate?" Paulina asked.

"He is my friend, I know him more than you do. He always uses women and dumps them." Paulina was shocked and speechless hearing what was coming out from Rufus's mouth about Ian.

"I'm very sorry I didn't tell you this earlier on," Rufus said.

"You need more than a 'sorry' about this matter," Paulina replied with annoyance. "I have told you that Kate is my sister, if anything happens to her through Ian, do you think that I'm going to forgive you?"

Rufus felt bad about the situation and said, "What could we do now to stop him? Do you want to call her and tell her?"

"No thank you, I'm not going to ruin her date simply because you failed to tell me about the matter earlier on," she replied. Paulina and Rufus's outing wasn't going well because Paulina was worrying about what might happen to Kate. She knew Kate was a clever lady but she was weak when she was intoxicated with alcohol. Rufus did not blame Kate at all, he blamed himself for not telling Kate about the situation earlier. When Paulina returned home she try to get hold of Kate through her mobile phone, but Kate's mobile phone was switched off.

Kate and Ian got on well on their date. Kate even promised to see Ian the next weekend. Despite the fact that Rufus didn't approve of Ian's suggestion, Ian tried to get his way with Kate. On the next morning, Paulina came to knock on Kate's door because she was worried she might be drunk and Ian could take advantage of her. Fortunately, Kate wasn't drunk at all. She'd only drunk a little wine when she was with Ian. But Ian really impressed her by telling her about his own life, how he flirted with women and how he dumped them. Now he wanted to change and be with only one woman. Kate was moved because she wasn't expecting Ian to be saying all this to her; he could keep it secret to himself until she became his victim. Kate was impressed that Ian was telling the truth and promised to see him again.

When Paulina knocked on Kate's door, Kate opened it and Paulina came in. "How was your date with Rufus?" Kate asked.

"It was fine, thank you. What about you with Ian?"

"It was fantastic," Kate replied in a happy mood.

"I hope he is not taking advantage of your drinking to get closer to you," Paulina said. Kate burst into laughter and said, "Are you telling me that I'm an alcoholic?"

Paulina looked at Kate in a funny way as she was talking. Kate moved towards Paulina where she sat, and looked into her eyes and said, "I'm not addicted to alcohol." Paulina burst into laughter.

"What are you laughing at? What brings all this nonsense? Is it because I went out with Ian?" Kate asked.

"Yes, because he is a slapper," Paulina replied.

Kate laughed for some seconds and replied, "He is not. You may think that I do not know anything about him, you are wrong. He told me about his life history. How he was sleeping with different women and dumping them. I don't think it concerns you whether he is a slapper or not, let me deal with the situation because it is my problem."

Paulina was surprised to hear that Ian had told Kate all his life history. She apologised to Kate and said, "You know that I'm really concerned about you."

"I know." Kate tapped her cheek with her right hand in a happy mood and said, "I can take care of myself."

They both went to the kitchen to prepare their breakfast. In the kitchen Paulina said, "It seems to me that Rufus is taking our relationship more seriously than we thought."

"Do you mean he wants to marry you?" Kate asked.

Paulina paused for some seconds and Kate looked at her eyes with a smile. "I think so," she said.

"Are you happy with him?" asked Kate.

"Yes, he makes me feel secure, comfortable and I am myself anytime I'm with him," she replied.

"Are you going to marry him before you finish your degree?" Kate asked.

"No, I have to finish my degree first before anything at all. Even if I wanted to do that, are you going to allow me?" Paulina replied.

"So far you are happy with him, you could take your time. But know that I am always there for you if you are ready," said Kate.

Paulina looked at Kate's eyes with a smile and replied, "Come here and give me a hug". Kate cuddled Paulina and Paulina said, "You are my sister, I love you."

"I love you too," Kate replied.

After breakfast Paulina said, "Let me go and have some rest before he starts to call."

Kate looked at Paulina's eyes with a smile and said, "I can see that you are committed to each other." Immediately Kate finished talking, Paulina's mobile phone rang. Paulina looked at the phone screen and saw Rufus's number.

"It's him, I told you" she said.

"I will see you later."

As Paulina went to answer the phone, the line went off. She redialled the number to speak to Rufus. "Why did you cut off the line?" she asked.

"The phone was ringing, you did not answer the phone," he replied.

"I was talking to Kate when you rang and I did not want to cut off the conversation. I'm sorry," she said.

"That is okay," he replied. "Anyway how are you?"

.

"I'm fine, thank you," she replied.

"I'm on the way to my room now; do you want us to see each other in the evening?"

"That would be great," she replied.

"Okay then I will see you in the evening."

"Bye, bye, she said.

The following week, Kate and Ian went for a drink. Their relationship developed from there and they started dating each other. As the relationship developed, Ian wanted commitment but Kate did not want to commit herself, because she wasn't sure whether Ian was the right person. She tried to explain this to Ian without damaging their relationship. Ian wasn't listening; he thought Kate didn't love him. Any time they sat down to resolved this issue, it always led to arguments. There was a day when Ian walked out, and finished with Kate. Kate later went to him and begged him and the relationship continued again. Although Kate loved Ian, the only thing she wasn't sure of was whether to marry him. When all this was going on between Kate and Ian, Kate refused to tell Paulina. Any time Paulina and Kate discussed Kate and Ian's affair, Kate always protected Ian. Paulina was so happy that Kate and Ian were happy together.

The problem of Kate and Ian's relationship started to affect Kate's education. Sometimes she would not turn up for the lesson. She and Paulina would leave home at the same time to the school but she would make an excuse that she was going to have words with Ian. Or sometimes she would say she was going to the library to borrow books. Paulina started to be suspicious of Kate's behaviour and her reactions. She knew that something was bothering her.

One day on the way to lesson, Kate said she needed to have words with one of her lecturers, and she would meet Paulina in the class. Paulina looked at her eyes and said, "Kate what is the matter?"

"Nothing," she replied.

Paulina was angry and held her hand and said with anger, "How long are you going to keep secrets from me? I'm your sister; tell me what is on your mind."

Kate looked at Paulina's eyes and burst into tears. Paulina cuddled her and said, "Don't cry, I'm here for you. I love you".

"I'm dying in silence," Kate said as she was crying.

"Do not say anything at the moment, let us go to our lesson first and after we will talk about it," Paulina said. Kate stopped crying and they went to their lesson.

After the lesson, Paulina took Kate to the nearby restaurant to have lunch. Paulina was doing this in order to make Kate calm down a little bit before she could talk to her. As they were eating Kate thanked Paulina for realising her problem.

"What are you thanking me for?" Paulina said. "After all, if anything happened to you, I would be the first person your family and my family would blame."

Kate looked at Paulina's eyes as she was talking, her emotion running high, and tears dropped from her eyes. Paulina cuddled her and tapped her on her back. "Do not cry," she said.

"I'm sorry that I've involved you in my problem," Kate said.

"That is alright, we're supposed to support each other as sisters," Kate wanted to continue talking. Paulina decided not to say anything until they got home. Kate stopped crying and continued with her food. Paulina looked at her face and smiled at her. Kate was delighted that Paulina was there for her. After they finished their lunch they went to Paulina's room. On the way to Paulina's room, Kate start to crack a joke with Paulina about the first day she met Rufus. Paulina was laughing and said, "I thought he was an arrogant guy because of the way he talked to me that day. But today I'm with him, happy and feel secure. Although I was upset that day, you are the one who calmed me down. I should be thanking you for your effort."

"What are you going to thank me for?" Kate replied.

"For making Rufus available for me," she said.

Kate burst into laughter and replied, "My sister, you were in the right place at the right time. You need to thank God, who made you and him compatible with each other,"

"My joy will be completed if we get married," Paulina said.

"Surely by the grace of God it will come to pass," Kate replied.

"Do you need a drink?" Paulina asked.

"A glass of wine would be better to cool my nerves down," Kate replied.

Paulina opened a bottle of red wine and poured it into two glasses. She gave a glass to Kate and raised her glass and said, "Cheers."

Kate looked at Paulina's face with a smile and replied, "Cheers". They both sat down to drink their wine for about five minutes.

Paulina said "Do you want to tell me what really happened to you when you were trying to avoid the lesson?"

Kate replied with a funny voice, "My nerves have calmed down now, I can talk to you, my sister."

Paulina burst into laughter and said, "I'm very happy that you are ready to talk."

"Do you know that you warned me about Ian before I started going out with him?"

"Yes, I do," Paulina replied.

Kate shook her head and said, "I should have listened to your advice,"

"Do you mean he has dumped you?" Paulina asked.

"No, if he had dumped me, it might have been better," Kate replied.

Paulina was trying to ask a question, but with a low voice, "You mean he asked you to marry him?" Kate shook her head up and down. Paulina paused for some seconds and asked, "Is that the reason why you were trying to avoid the lesson?"

"Yes, I couldn't cope with it," Kate said.

"Did you say no to him?" Paulina asked.

"Yes, because I am not sure whether he is the right man for me to marry," she said.

"Do you love him?" Paulina asked.

"Yes, I love him, and I do not want to lose him. But I'm not ready for a serious relationship at the moment. I have my education to think about at present and I don't want anything that could disturb my attention and make me not focus on my education."

"I can see that you have a genuine point but how did he take it? " Paulina asked.

"He was very annoyed and said I do not love him. He even said to me that he was finished with me. I had to beg him before we reconciled."

"How long this thing has been going on?" Paulina asked.

"More than two months," Kate replied.

"Why couldn't you tell me?" Paulina asked.

"I didn't want to drag you in to my mess," Kate replied.

Paulina shook her head from left to right. "Why are you shaking your head?" Kate asked.

Paulina moved closer to Kate and looked at her face and said, "Do you accept me as your sister?"

"Yes I do," Kate replied.

"Why, when something has been bothering you, you did not want to tell me, until I discovered by myself," Paulina said.

Kate smiled and replied with an honourable voice, "I thought I could handle it by myself before, but I was wrong. Please, I'm sorry."

"Now, what do you think we should do about this problem?" Paulina said.

"I don't even have a clue," Kate replied.

"Do you know you need to be strong for yourself in order to combat this problem. By avoiding lessons it does not do you any good," Paulina said.

Kate looked at Paulina's face as she was talking and held her hands and said, "I feel strong now as I told you the problem. I know that you are always there for me. But you need to help me overcome this problem. I cannot do it by myself."

Paulina cuddled her and said, "We are going to do it together. If you tell him your condition and he refuses totally, you leave him and concentrate on your education."

"Thank you very much," Kate said.

"Finish your drink, let us stroll out to the university compound," Paulina said.

Kate poured her drink into her mouth and said with a happy mood, "Let us go."

Paulina and Kate went to the university compound. Paulina's aim was to talk to Ian about Kate's matter but she instructed her not to do so. As they were strolling around the university compound, Paulina's mobile rang. Paulina looked at her mobile screen and see that Rufus was the one that was calling. She answered the call. "Where are you?" Rufus asked.

"I'm in the university compound with Kate." Paulina replied.

"Wait for me, I will meet you there," he said.

"Okay, bye, bye", Paulina replied. Kate looked at Paulina's face and smiled.

"What is that smile for?" Paulina asked.

"I could see that you have no problem with your fiancé," Kate replied.

"I have told you several times that he makes me believe myself, and I am comfortable," Paulina said.

"Do you think it's because you agreed to marry him?" said Kate.

"I don't know, but he is the type of guy I could spend the rest of my life with."

Kate paused for some seconds, then with a smile she said, "That is the different between my relationship with Ian and yours. You are sure of being with Rufus for the rest of your life. But I'm not sure about Ian yet, although he's treating me nicely. He needs to give me more time to be sure of myself. I don't want to rush into anything at the moment, so that I will not regret it in the end."

Paulina wanted to start talking, but as Rufus appeared, she stopped. Rufus kissed Paulina and said, "Kate, how are you?"

"I'm fine, thank you" Kate replied. "The only problem I have at the moment is with your friend Ian."

"Did he give you a hard time?" Rufus asked.

"No, he just wants me to marry him, that's all," she replied.

"Marry!" Rufus squeezed his face. "That means he has turned over a new leaf."

Kate looked at Paulina's eyes, smiling. Then Paulina said, "You know him better than we do. Do you think he is not serious about the marriage?"

"This is my first time hearing that Ian wants someone to marry him since I've known him."

Paulina looked at Kate eyes, smiling, and said, "Do you mean that Kate must be special to him?"

"I think so," Rufus replied, nodding his head up and down.

"Kate, I think the ball is in your court," Paulina said.

"I have told you my mind, I'm not sure whether he's the right person for me," Kate replied.

"Do you mean you are not ready for commitment now?" Rufus asked.

"Yes, I want to concentrate on my degree first, then after that I could think of something else," replied Kate.

Rufus looked at Paulina's eyes and Paulina replied with a smile. Before Rufus could say anything at all, Kate intervened. "I do not want you to have bad impression that I do not love him. I do love him, but I'm not ready for serious commitment at the moment".

"What do you want me to do now?" Rufus asked.

"You need to talk to him and let him realise that I do love him but I'm not ready for marriage at this time," Kate replied.

"Do you mean if he could wait until you finish your degree you could make the decision?" Paulina intervened.

"Yes I would be very glad if he could wait," Kate replied.

"Okay, I will talk to him," Rufus said.

Rufus kissed Paulina and cuddled Kate and said, "I will see you later."

Kate was so relieved that Rufus was going to talk to Ian on her behalf. "But if Rufus talks to him and he doesn't listen, what are you going to do?" Paulina asked.

"We'll have to split up," she replied.

Rufus talked to Ian, but he refused to listen to him. Ian called Kate on her mobile and told her that their relationship was finished. Rufus blamed himself for talking to Ian and the way Ian had reacted to the whole issue. Meanwhile Kate told Rufus not to bother about her split up with Ian.

Ian tried to avoid Kate at all costs, but Kate wanted them to be friends. Kate asked Paulina to talk to Ian so that they could become friends. Ian agreed on friendship with Kate, knowing that he had something in his mind for her.

The break-up of the relationship between Kate and Ian affected Kate but she was able to get over it with the help of her friend Paulina. Any time Kate felt lonely, Paulina and Rufus would take her out either to a restaurant or club. The worst thing was that Kate saw Ian almost every day and when she saw him the guilty conscience came to her mind that she was the one that had caused the breakdown of their relationship. But Ian didn't think of that, instead he was thinking how he was going to punish Kate on their last day at university.

Kate decided not to have another boyfriend because she was in her final year. Rather, she concentrated on her studies in order to have good grades. Although Paulina respected Kate's wishes, she advised Kate that she was too young to stay without a boyfriend. Maybe Paulina thought that as it had worked for her to get a perfect man, Kate could also do the same. Kate told Paulina that she didn't want to rush anything at moment.

After a couple of months, before their final exam, Ian told Martin and Johnson that they should rape Kate. Martin disagreed with the suggestion because he thought that Ian was wrong to punish Kate for their break up. But Johnson asked Ian how he was going to do it. Ian came up with his plan that he would organise a send off party and he would invite Kate and drug her.

"What if Paulina comes with her to the party?" Johnson asked "What are you going to do?"

"Before the party I will have a misunderstanding with Rufus to discourage him and Paulina from turning up," Ian replied.

"But how are you going to invite Kate, when you have already broken up with her?" Martin asked.

"When we start our final exams I will get closer to her and pretend that I want to come back," replied Ian. They both laughed and Johnson said, "You are a crooked man."

A week before their exam, Ian bombarded Kate with calls on her mobile, that they should settle their grievances and start afresh. Kate told Paulina about Ian's calls and what he had said. Paulina was delighted for Kate because she knew Kate really loved Ian. Throughout their separation, Kate always spoke about Ian. Kate said to Ian she could not say anything at the moment because she was concentrating on her exam, but if she finished her exam, she would talk to him. Ian was happy about Kate's reply because he knew she was going to attend the party. When they started their exam, Ian went to Kate all the time. They did reading together throughout their examination period.

But Kate did not allow Ian to touch her. Ian didn't make any attempt simply because he knew what his aim was. Kate was surprised that Ian did not even make an attempt to touch her. But Ian always said to her, "I don't want to rush you, I want you to concentrate on your exam." Kate thought all these statements Ian was telling her were genuine and he was serious about their reunion. Kate even told Paulina what Ian was doing and Paulina also believed that Ian was serious about coming back.

On the day of the final exam, Ian met Kate on his way to the library to return some of the books he had borrowed.

"Kate, how are you doing?" he asked.

"I'm doing fine, thank you."

"Are you nervous about the last paper?" he asked.

"Students are always nervous about their examinations, as you know," Kate replied.

"There is one thing I wanted to tell you before but

because you are so focused on your examination I was unable to tell you," Ian said.

"What is that you cannot tell me, since all these days we have been doing revision together?" she replied.

Ian knew that he and his friends could only execute their plan if Kate agreed to come to the party. Ian took a deep breath.

"What is it?" Kate asked.

"My friends and I are organising a send off party after the last paper."

Kate replied, "Please don't let us talk about parties at moment, we will discuss that after our paper."

Ian said goodbye to Kate and promised to talk to her after their paper. Now Ian started to have doubts whether Kate would attend the party. He kept this to himself because if Martin and Johnson knew about it they might laugh at him and discourage him from his plan.

After the paper Kate was in a good mood because she had done well in her exam. With anxiety she went to Paulina and they discussed their performances in the exam.

As Kate and Paulina were talking, Rufus came and joined them and they all talked about the exam, and how they had been working hard for it, and they deserved good results. Kate remembered that Ian had been talking to her about a send off party after the paper. She asked Paulina and Rufus whether they would attend the party. Rufus declined and said Ian hadn't told him about the party and he had engaged himself with other friends. They were going to a club that day. But if they left the club they might come and meet them at the party. Kate looked at Paulina's eyes and said, "That is great." She left Paulina and Rufus and went to look for Ian. Kate saw Ian, Martin and

Johnson discussing their party.

"Kate, how are you doing?" Martin asked.

"I'm doing well," she replied.

"I can see a smile on your face," Johnson intervened.

"I'm just happy about the exam and how it goes," she said.

"That means our hard work for the revision proved positive," Ian said.

"Yes, I suppose," she replied. They both smiled at each other and Kate said, "You were talking to me earlier about a party. I was not in a good enough mood to listen to you."

"What can I say?" Ian said, grumbling.

Johnson and Martin looked at each other and concentrated on what Kate was going to say, which would determine the outcome of their plan.

"I'm sorry not to listen to you. Now what do you want me to do about the party?"

Ian smiled and looked at Martin and Johnson and said, "What do you want her to do?"

"She can bring some spirit if she can afford it," Johnson said.

Ian wanted to say that would be too expensive for her, but Kate intervened. "That is alright, I will bring some."

"Thank you very much, Kate," Ian said.

"What about Paulina and Rufus, have you told them?" Martin asked.

"I have told them but they were already engaged that day. They promised me that they would come to meet me at the party if it was not too late for them."

Ian looked at Martin and Johnson's faces and they responded with smiles. This is because they both knew that if Paulina and Rufus came to the party, it would not be possible for them to execute their plan. There was nothing they could do than to keep their fingers crossed. Martin and Johnson departed. Ian thanked Kate for accepting his invitation to the party and also for volunteering to bring some spirits. After Ian said goodbye to Kate, he went to meet Martin and Johnson.

On the day of the party, Kate helped Ian and his friend to entertain the visitors by serving them drinks. Kate was also happy that the pressure of examinations was gone and she needed to enjoy herself for the last time. As she was serving the visitors she was trying to enjoying herself by getting drunk. Ian and his friends pretended that they were drunk, but they were not. In the middle of the night, when everybody was drunk and enjoying the party music, Ian called Kate outside to talk to her about their relationship.

Despite Kate being, drunk she was comfortable to be talking to Ian outside the party venue because she thought that this was the chance to be back together again. But this was not what was in Ian's mind. After their discussion, Kate kissed Ian and Ian couldn't resist. They both went inside for more drink. Martin and Johnson were watching Ian in case he changed his mind. This was because they saw Ian and Kate kissing each other outside the party venue. They approached Ian to see whether he had changed his mind, but Ian said 'No'. About 3 o'clock in the morning, people started to leave the party because Ian had booked the venue till 3.30 am. Kate wanted to go because she was heavily drunk, but Ian asked her to wait, that he would escort her home. Kate agreed to Ian's demand.

Kate waited outside in the fresh air while Ian, Martin and Johnson tried to collect the remaining drinks. When Martin came outside for fresh air he saw Kate being sick on the floor. He went inside to call Ian; Ian came out to attend to Kate. He gave her water to drink and also to wash her mouth. As Ian was caring for Kate because she was heavily drunk, Kate looked at Ian's eyes with emotion and started kissing him. They both kissed each other. Johnson came out and saw Ian and Kate kissing each other, he took a picture with his mobile and went in to show the picture to Martin. Ian pretended that he loved Kate as they were kissing each other.

After they had all finished tidying up, Ian, Martin and Johnson escorted Kate to her room where they raped her. Although Kate was heavily drunk, she was aware what was going on, and she couldn't help herself. After she woke up, she was very, very angry with herself and continue to ask herself the question, why had she got so drunk?

Kate promised to keep this to herself, not to tell anybody, but to accuse Ian, Martin and Johnson. Paulina was worried about Kate and she came to knock her door. Fortunately, Kate had taken her bath when Paulina visited her.

"How was the party, Kate?" asked Paulina.

"The party was great," she replied.

"I'm very sorry that we couldn't make it," Paulina said.

"That is alright" everybody just enjoyed themselves," Kate replied.

"Did you and Ian finally come together?" she asked.

"What do you mean by 'come together,' Paulina?" Kate asked.

Paulina wanted to start talking, but Kate excused herself to go to the toilet. She locked the door and wept bitterly because of what Ian and his friends had done to her. Kate used tissue to wipe the tears in her eyes as she looked in the mirror. She could see flashbacks of Ian and his friends raping her.

Kate came out from the toilet to meet Paulina in the

kitchen and they both prepared food and ate. After breakfast, Paulina and Kate discussed how they needed to go and see their parents in the countryside before they both decided what to do next. As they were discussing, Paulina's phone rang.

"That is him, Paulina," Kate said. She looked at Paulina's face and smiling, said, "Is that Rufus?"

"Yes, you know," she replied.

Immediately Paulina answered the call and she said to Kate, "I have to go now, I'll see you later."

"Is there a problem?" Kate asked.

"No, he just needs to go some place," replied Paulina. Paulina opened the door and left. Kate was full of anger in her stomach, and she set out to go and confront Ian and his friends aboutwhat they had done to her. She first called Ian on his phone. When Ian noticed it was Kate calling, he turned off his mobile. But Kate was determined to look for him before he left the campus. Kate went straight to the men's dormitory to knock on Ian's door, but he was not at home. As Kate was about to leave the gate she saw Martin and he dodged so Kate wouldn't see him. Kate pursued him and shouted his name, "Martin, Martin". He stopped and waited for Kate, to hear what she was going to say. When Kate came closer, Martin squeezed his face and pretended that he was serious. Then Kate said, "You bastard, I saw what you and your friends did to me last night. And I swear to God that you and your friends will pay the price."

"What are you going to do now?" Martin asked. "Are you going to call the police?"

Kate was so annoyed that Martin asked her that type of question, that she replied with anger, You bastard, I will think what I will do to you and your friends."

With anger, Kate turned away from Martin to look for Ian. As she was going, Martin said, "Sorry, it was not my fault". Kate turned back to Martin and touched him in the chest with her finger and said ,"Better sorry for yourself. You and your friends! Your heads will roll."

Martin replied again, "I'm sorry, not my fault."

With anger, she asked, "Whose fault is it?"

Martin felt reluctant to talk, then Kate came closer to him and touched him in his chest again and repeatedly said, "Say something, say something."

Martin opened his mouth and said, "Ian planned the whole thing."

"Why did he do that to me?" she asked, with tears in her eyes. She repeated the same words several times.

Martin replied, "He said he wanted to punish you for you for refusing to marry him the time he proposed to you".

With tears Kate replied, "But I did not refuse to marry him, I just said I needed to concentrate on my degree first, after that I would be able to decide."

Martin was moved by what Kate said, because Ian had not told him the entire story. He had just said to Martin and Johnson that Kate had refused to marry him and he was going to punish her. Martin moved closer to Kate in order to cuddle her so that she would stop crying. Kate was annoyed and said, "Don't touch me, you bastard" and left.

Kate was going to her dormitory, with anger, to sit down and reason why Ian had planned to rape her. She saw Johnson with some ladies in the restaurant, drinking wine. She went there straight away without caring about anybody, and she said to Johnson with anger, "I want to have a word with you". The ladies sitting down with Johnson were embarrassed, but Johnson excused himself and followed Kate, simply because he knew what he had done to her, and he didn't want Kate to shout at him in the presence of the ladies.

When they came to an open place, Kate said with anger, "You bastard, I saw what you and your friends did to me."

As Kate was talking, tears dropped from her eyes. "Did I deserve this?" she said. "What have I done to you and your friends?" she asked.

"It wasn't my plan at all."

"But why didn't you advise him not to do it?"

"He was determined to go alone," he replied.

With anger Kate said, "Why couldn't you refuse to join him?"

"I'm sorry for what I have done, because he said he wanted to punish you for refusing to marry him,"

"What I said to him was I cannot commit myself now because I need to finish my degree before thinking of commitment."

Johnson was shocked to hear what Kate said. He deeply regretted that Ian had brainwashed him to do a bad thing.

"What are you going to do now?" Johnson asked.

"I just want to talk to Ian and ask him why he has done this to me."

Kate walked away from Johnson. "I am sorry," he said.

"Sorry for yourself," Kate replied.

Kate was totally confused whether to tell the whole matter to Paulina or not. But in her mind she still wanted to talk to Ian. That very day Kate was unable to talk to Ian. She tried his mobile several times but it was switched off. Kate delivered several messages to Ian's voicemail and asked him to contact her if he heard the message. Despite the fact that Ian heard the message, he did not return the call. Meanwhile Johnson went to Ian after he left Kate.

"Ian, we're in trouble," he said.

"What is the matter?" Ian replied.

"Kate knew that we raped her and she is looking for you," said Johnson.

"Is that what you are concerned about? But that was our plan, to rape her," Ian replied.

Johnson was annoyed with the way Ian talked to him and said with anger, "It was not our plan, it was your plan." He moved closer to Ian and pointing fingers in his face, he said, "You lied to us that Kate refused to marry you, and that is why you wanted to punish her."

"Yes, it is true she refused to marry me," replied Ian.

"You bloody liar, I was just talking to Kate not more than five minutes ago and she said she wanted to concentrate on her degree first before anything.".

"Is that what she told you?" Ian said.

"Yes," he replied.

"I do not have any comment, and I do not want to discuss this matter again," said Ian. He went to turn away from Johnson with anger , but Johnson grabbed his shirt and said, "Is that all with anger, your voice? After you have involved us in your bloody plan by lying to us."

As Ian was about to open his mouth, Johnson punched his mouth and blood rushed out. Ian was furious about Johnson's attitude, but Johnson did not show any concern at all. Johnson left with anger and went to Martin's room. Johnson knocked on Martin's door and Martin opened the door, feeling low.

"Why do you feel so low, Martin?" Johnson asked.

"Have you seen Ian?" he said.

"Yes, why do you ask about him?" Johnson asked.

"I want to have a word with him," replied Martin.

"Is it because of the Kate matter?" Johnson said.

"Yes", he replied.

"I just left him with blood in his nose," said Johnson.

"Do you mean you punched him hard?" Martin said with a smile on his face.

"Yes, because he is a bloody liar," he replied.

"Did Kate talk to you?" Martin asked.

"Yes, I feel ashamed of myself for participating in that type of idiotic behaviour," Johnson replied.

"She also talked to me earlier on," Martin said. "I couldn't believe myself that Ian was lying to us. Now what has happened has happened, how can we make up with Kate before we go to our different destinations?" Martin said.

"The way I saw her earlier on I think she was so annoyed. Even if we try to talk to her she might not want to talk to us," replied Johnson.

"Do you mean we should depart with this guilt in our minds?" Martin asked.

"Nothing we can do about it, we have already made fools of ourselves. We should live with the guilt for the rest of our lives," Johnson replied.

Meanwhile, on that day Kate did not see Ian to talk to. She was troubled in her mind that Ian might leave without her seeing him. She decided to look for him the next morning.

Fortunately for Kate, as she was going to buy breakfast in the nearest restaurant because she didn't feel like eating at home, she saw Ian in the restaurant eating breakfast. She was annoyed and shouted at him, "I need to talk to you." . To the people eating it was a shock, but Ian, as he knew what he had done, stood up quietly and followed her outside. Kate grabbed Ian's shirt and said, "You bastard."

"What have I done to you?" she repeated several times. Ian was silent because he thought Kate would call the police to arrest him. Kate looked at his eyes and shook her head and said, "It isn't worth calling the police on you and your friends, because you lied to them to involve them in your bloody behaviour. If I call the police it will affect them also, but I pray to God that you will reap whatever you have sown."

Kate left Ian and went to her dormitory to meet Paulina. Immediately Paulina saw Kate, she could see that something was troubling her.

"Kate, what is the matter?" Paulina asked.

"Nothing," Kate replied.

"By looking at your face it doesn't appear to me that nothing is wrong," Paulina said.

"I just had a quarrel with Ian in the restaurant," Kate replied.

"Why? Both of you were getting on well before our final exam, which you yourself confirmed. What is the matter now?"

Kate kept silent as Paulina was talking. Paulina looked at her eyes and said, "Do you have anything to tell me?"

Kate smiled and replied, "There's nothing to tell."

"Is it because of this marriage problem again?" asked Paulina.

"Yes, my sister," Kate replied, smiling. "But everything is settled now. I can have peace of mind."

Paulina looked at Kate with a sideways look , but before she could say another word, Kate intervened.

"Meaning, I'm dumping him." They both laughed and Kate was feeling great despite not wanting to reveal the truth about the matter to Paulina.

Martin and Johnson were troubled in their minds because of this matter. They sent text messages to Kate to apologise that Ian had been able to convince them to do this terrible thing.

Kate and Paulina went to the countryside to see their parents before their next moves after their graduation. While Rufus stayed in the capital, he promised Paulina that he would visit her with his parents.

Martin and Johnson weren't talking to Ian before they departed to their destination. They promised each other that they would be in touch. Ian wasn't sure what Kate might do next, he was troubled in his mind. After he learned that Paulina and Kate had gone to the countryside to see their parents, he was a little bit relieved.

Rufus and his parents visited Paulina's family. Paulina was delighted to see Rufus's parents. After Rufus's parents' visit, Paulina decided to move in with Rufus in the capital, and it was approved by Paulina's family. Two months later Kate also moved to the capital and got a job at a departmental store as a manager. Paulina and Rufus got a teaching job in the same secondary school.

Kate did not associate with men in the working place, because of the effect of the rape on her. She also refused to go out for a drink with them. Anytime she had a flashback of the rape, she would go to the toilet and weep. Although Kate tried hard not to remember the incident, she couldn't help herself. She also decided not to touch anything containing alcohol.

Kate's contacted Paulina and Rufus by phone until they got married. Paulina and Rufus's wedding was attended by Kate and Paulina's parents. Both Paulina and Kate's families were delighted that their dream had come true. They even cracked a joke with Kate and Paulina about what they said they were going to be when they grew up.

The memory of the rape was still with Kate, and as a result she planned what to do to men in order to get revenge. She started collecting magazines about celebrities. Kate realised for her to carry out her plan she needed money. Although she was working hard, after paying her loan from the university and house rent, her salary remained too little for her to save.

Kate's first step was to undergo plastic surgery to boost her image, and because she couldn't save enough she got a part-time job as an assistant manager in fashion design. The whole year Kate was working, she wasn't buying anything for her accommodation. She only bought second hand furniture and a few clothes she could wear to work. The rest of the money went into her account. Kate was working hard to save money, and she also opened a file for those married celebrities she wanted to deal with, cut their picture out and put it in the file. On the front page of the file she wrote:

"They rape me with smiles on their faces – but I will deal with them seriously. REVENGE."

Kate worked for two and a half years and saved enough money to undergo the first surgery. She called the clinic and spoke to the consultant, who gave her the date for consultation. The surgeon asked Kate why she wanted to enlarge her breasts. "I want to work as a TV presenter," Kate replied.

"Have you got a job with them?"

"No, I need to boost my image before I apply," she replied.

"Which means you are not going to do your breasts alone?"

"Yes doctor, you're right" she replied. "But I can only afford the breasts now before my face."

"Do you mean that it is money that delays you from getting the job you like?" the doctor said with a smile. He was joking with Kate.

Kate realised that the doctor was joking with her, and she asked for his advice.

"I would advise you not to do your face because you have a beautiful face and long hair. The breasts and the bottom could be a great boost to your image," the doctor said.

Kate stood up and turned round with a smile on her

face and said, "Do you mean that my bottom is flat?"

"No", he replied. "It would be great if you could enlarge it a little bit to match your beautiful long hair."

"You are on, doctor," Kate said. "I will give you a call the day I feel that it is convenient for me."

The doctor gave Kate his card and said, "Call me at anytime when you are ready."

"Thank you very much, doctor." Kate left.

Kate was delighted with the consultation because the surgeon gave her his opinion which Kate thought was perfect. "I will make all men who come my way pay for the sin Ian and his friends committed," Kate said in her mind on the way to her flat after the consultation.

At her work place Kate tried to isolate herself but deal with her staff professionally according to the company policy. Whether she was a manager or an assistant manager, she avoided making friends. Kate was doing all this to avoid questions when she started her operations.

After three months Kate went for a consultation for her breast enlargement. She was able to do this by taking two weeks holiday from both her jobs. Kate's first operation was successful and she was happy with her breasts. When Kate was leaving the clinic she promised the surgeon that she would come back for the bottom enlargement.

At home, every morning before Kate took her breakfast she would look at her collection file to remind her what she was going to do with married celebrities. Sometimes she even joked with her collection about the one she was going to deal with first and how she was going to get him.

After two weeks holiday Kate returned to work with boosted breasts. Although her workers noticed what had happened, they couldn't ask her. In her part-time job Kate's manager used her breasts to joke with her. But Kate wasn't annoyed, because her manager loved it. She even asked Kate to take her to her consultant for her to enlarge her own. Because of this Kate and her part-time work manager became friends. Three weeks later, Kate took her part-time manager to see the consultant. On the way home after seeing the consultant, Mandy, Kate's manager, said, "Kate, you look more beautiful than before."

"Thank you, Mandy," she replied. "I haven't finished with my body yet."

"Do you mean you're still going back for more operations?" she asked.

"Yes, Mandy," Kate replied.

Mandy laughed and looked at Kate with a sideways look and said, "Are you doing this because of your boyfriend?"

"No, I do not have anyone at the moment," Kate replied.

Mandy laughed. "Are you afraid of men?"

"No Mandy, I just want to have time for myself."

"You're right", Mandy said. "Sometimes it's better to live alone but you need someone to live with for the rest of your life. Now tell me about the next operation."

"I'm going to enlarge my bottom," Kate replied.

Mandy was amazed and asked "Do you want to be a Hollywood star?"

"That is my aim, Mandy," Kate replied.

"You're a beautiful lady with strong determination. I know that you can achieve your aim if you're serious about it."

"Thank you Mandy for your compliment," said Kate. "You yourself you're beautiful, Mandy. You could do the same if you wanted to," she said.

"I know that I am beautiful enough, but you cannot compare my beauty with yours," Mandy replied. Kate laughed. "Why are you laughing Kate" she asked.

"I do not consider myself as a beautiful lady," Kate replied.

"I'm serious Kate, you're beautiful," she said. "With your long hair and round face you will win the world if you could enlarge your bottom as you did your breasts."

Kate laughed and said, "What about you, Mandy?"

"I don't think my bottom needs enlargement, as you see, Kate I have already got enough," she replied. "Could we go to my flat for a cup of coffee if you don't mind?"

"That would be great," replied Kate.

On their way to Mandy's flat, Kate was joking with Mandy about how the manager and the assistant manager were trying to boost their breasts. Mandy was laughing and said, "I didn't know that you could be funny like this, Kate. At work you keep yourself to yourself and distant from other people."

"Sometimes you have to keep yourself to yourself if you do not want trouble because human beings are dangerous."

"You are right," Mandy said.

In Mandy's flat Kate looked around and saw that her flat was decorated nicely. "You must have spent a fortune on these decorations," she said.

"That is what I am working for," Mandy replied.

"How long have you been living in the flat?"

"About seven years I think," Mandy replied. "Formerly, I was living with my boyfriend."

"Do you mean in this flat?" Kate asked.

"Yes, of course," Mandy replied.

"Where is your boyfriend now?" asked Kate.

"He dumped me a year ago," she replied.

"M-e-n! They are full of trouble" Kate said. She looked at Mandy's eyes and said, "Let's forget about men and enjoy our coffee."

"You are right," Mandy replied.

Mandy and Kate became friends, visiting one another, although Kate kept her plan secret. Three months later Kate checked in for the second operation to enlarge her bottom. Mandy went with Kate and Kate was delighted.

After the operation Kate stayed at home for two weeks, which she took as holiday. The result of Kate's bottom enlargement was superb. The operation transformed Kate completely into glamorous lady. At her full time job nobody doubted that Kate was aiming at something. Her boss even talked to her in a polite manner about her image. But Kate didn't take it as offence, rather she tendered her resignation letter a week later. Kate resigned from her full time job to execute her plan, also she needed to furnish her flat. Kate talked to her bank manager and borrowed money to decorate her flat. When she was doing this she kept Mandy in the dark.

Although, she visited Mandy as usual, Mandy did not bother to visit her and she didn't complain. After Kate finished decorating her flat to her taste she said to Mandy on Friday at work, "Do you mind after work if we could visit my flat for a quick coffee?"

"Why not?" Mandy replied.

On the way to Kate's flat they went to the supermarket to buy some stuff. Kate picked up some wine and Mandy was surprised and said, "But you do not drink anything containing alcohol. What has happened? Have you won the lottery?"

Kate looked at her face and smiled. Mandy suspected that something was going on, the way Kate continued to smile.

When they got to Kate's flat, Kate opened the door and said, "Come in with good luck." Without seeing anything yet, Mandy replied, "You need it, my dear." When Mandy entered and saw how Kate had decorated and furnished her flat, she shouted, amazed, "I know that you are up to something," she said.

Kate looked at her eyes and replied, "I told you I want to be a TV presenter or a Hollywood star."

Mandy started to look round the flat with surprise. Kate opened a bottle of wine and poured it into two glasses and gave one to Mandy. Raising her own glass , she said, "A toast to Kate's future."

Mandy replied, "Cheers," but was still in shock.

After some glasses of wine, Kate prepared dinner and they both ate together. As they were eating the dinner Kate said, "Have you given up looking for a nice boyfriend?"

Mandy looked at Kate's eyes and replied, "No, because sometimes they are useful."

"What do you mean by useful?" she asked.

"I'm the type of person who wants to live a family life," Mandy replied.

"Oh, oh, that is why you use the word useful."

"Yes of course," Mandy replied.

"If you wanted to live family life you'd better do it in time because you are getting old," Kate said with a smile.

Mandy laughed. "What about you Kate, are you not getting old?" she asked.

"Yes of course," Kate replied, "But it not going to be easy for me to trust a man again."

"Have you had lots of bad experience with men?" Mandy asked.

Kate looked at her and smiled. Then Mandy continued, "I do not blame you, my dear, men are useless. Despite the fact that they are useless we still need them in our life."

As they finished the dinner Mandy said, "It's getting

late, I'd better start moving."

"Do you have plans for tomorrow?" Kate asked.

"Not really," Mandy replied.

"Why can't you sleep here and go tomorrow?" Kate asked.

"Do you mean we should continue our gossip?" Mandy said with a funny, deep voice.

Kate laughed and said, "That is funny, Mandy." They both laughed.

"I need a hot bath," Mandy said.

"Let me give you a towel," Kate said. She went to her room to bring a new towel. She threw the towel to Mandy and said, "Feel at home, my dear."

"This towel smells nice," Mandy said.

"I have kept it for Mr Right for such a long time," Kate replied with a funny voice. They both looked at each other and laughed and start to joke about Mr Right.

After Kate and Mandy finished showering they sat down in the living room watching some movies, with glass of wine in Mandy's hand and diet coke in Kate's glass. Mandy said, "It might have been better if we had a man with us here."

"Do you mean for me and you?" Kate replied.

"Yes of course," Mandy said with a smile.

Kate laughed and replied, "The man would have had a hard lot of job to satisfy me and you."

They both kept silent and concentrated on the movies for about five minutes.

Kate said, "Mandy, sorry to ask you this question again. What really happened between you and your boyfriend before he left you?"

"It is a long story, Kate," Mandy replied.

Kate sat down properly and said, "Tell me Mandy, I want to hear about it."

Mandy looked at her face and smiled and replied,

"Why not? I met him when I was doing a placement with a financial bank. Although the relationship wasn't serious at that time, I wanted to go back to university to finish my degree. I thought that if I left the company to finish my degree, that would the end. But he started bombarding me with flowers and letters when I went back to school."

Kate intervened. "That sounds romantic to me."

Mandy looked at Kate's eyes with a smile and replied, "He also helped me financially during my time in the university. I was not borrowing money from the bank, which really helped me to save after my degree."

"He must be a nice guy then," Kate said.

"Yes, he was. That is why I decided to live with him after my education. He even gave me a job in his company."

"Do you mean the same company you did the placement in?"

"Yes," Mandy replied.

"Why did you leave the job? You could have been getting better money than the one you are doing now."

"I was getting good money, but it was not what I really wanted to do," replied Mandy.

"What was in your mind at that time?"

"I wanted to work in the fashion and design business," she replied. Kate laughed and laughed. "Why are you laughing?" Mandy asked.

"Nothing," Kate replied and poured some coke into her mouth.

"Despite that, it was not what I wanted, but I stayed in the job because I loved him. Not only that, I saw him all the time. We finished at the same time and came home together."

"If you enjoyed all these things, why didn't you stay?" Kate intervened.

Mandy paused for a few seconds. With a smile she

replied, "I quit the job because I couldn't take it anymore."

"Do you mean the stress in the job?" Kate asked.

Kate said, "No, when he started taking drugs."

Kate took deep breath and asked, "Why couldn't you talk to him?"

"I talked to him but he wasn't listening. He promised me several times that he was going to stop, but he did not. I even booked an appointment for him to see a counsellor. He went twice and stopped without letting me know."

"Did the drugs affect him at work?" Kate asked.

"No, his boss liked him because he was a hard working person."

"Did his boss know about his condition?"

"Of course, he even called him and talked to him several times, but he wasn't listening. I could have been with him despite his drug problem but he was so violent at home anytime I talked to him about the drugs."

"What do you mean by violent?" asked Kate with a harsh voice.

Mandy paused for some seconds and tears dropped from her eyes. Kate moved closer to her and placed her hand on Mandy's shoulder and rubbed her back with her right hand. Mandy took a deep breath and said, "That's better." Kate gave her a tissue to clean her eyes. She looked at Kate's face and replied, smiling, "Thank you Kate." she

"What are you thanking me for?" Kate asked.

"For listening to me," she said.

"I can see the reason why you left the job, but why did he leave his flat for you instead of you moving out?"

Mandy smiled and with a cool voice she replied, "It's my flat, not his flat."

"But you said to me before that you moved in with him after your degree."

"Yes," Mandy replied. "Because of his violence I moved out of his flat and got my own flat. Later he begged me and promised heaven and earth, and that he was going to listen to me. He also agreed to counselling, that is why I took him back. He moved in with me and kept his promises for only four months before he started again. The worst thing he did, the day I asked him to move out." Mandy paused.

"He stole your money?" Kate intervened by looking at Mandy's eyes.

Mandy shook her head left to right and tears dropped from her eyes.

"No, No, do not tell me he raped you," Kate said. Mandy nodded her head up and down and cried loudly. Kate cuddled her and said, "Don't cry Mandy, men are bastards."

After Mandy regained herself, Kate did not want them to continue the conversation . She said, "Let us go to bed Mandy, we will finish our gossip tomorrow."

"You're right Kate, its bedtime," Mandy replied.

In the morning Kate went to the kitchen to prepare two cups of tea for them to drink before their breakfast. "Mandy, wake up! Here is your tea," Kate said.

"Thank you, Kate. I really need one to keep me awake," Mandy replied. Mandy sat on the bed while Kate sat on the chair enjoying her tea.

"How are you feeling this morning Mandy?"

"I'm fine. Thank you for your hospitality," Mandy replied with a smile. "What about you Kate?"

"I'm great with this cup of tea."

Kate switched on the bedroom television with the remote control in her hand. There was a children's programme going on. "Could you put on Sky News please?" Mandy asked.

Immediately Kate changed the channel. On Sky News there was news about a man who had raped a woman. Kate was so upset that she switched off the television. Mandy could see the anger on her face but she kept silent. After a couple of minutes, Mandy switched on the television again. By this time the rape news had gone. Mandy wanted to ask Kate why she was so upset about the rape news, after all she was the one whose boyfriend had raped her. But she feared upsetting her more.

"Please could we go and prepare our breakfast?" Mandy asked with a funny voice. Kate looked at her eyes with a smile and replied, "I'm starving." They both went to the kitchen for their breakfast. As they were eating, Kate looked at Mandy's face across the table. "I know that you will be wondering why I switched off the television," she said.

Mandy took a deep breath, looked at Kate's eyes, and she replied, "I did not want to upset you more, I could have asked the reason. I was thinking I should be the one to be upset because of the story I told you yesterday."

"Do you mean about your boyfriend?" Kate replied.

"Yes." Kate paused for some seconds as she looked up at Mandy's eyes, and tears dropped from her own eyes. Mandy stopped eating to comfort Kate, but Kate couldn't control her emotions, tears dropped from her eyes as she was crying. After some minutes Kate looked at Mandy's eyes and she saw that she was also crying. They both cuddled each other and started laughing. "Men are bastards," they both said.

After breakfast they went to the living room with their nightgowns on. "Mandy are you sure you do not have any plans today?" Kate asked.

"No my dear, I just want to relax myself for the weekend."

After some minutes Mandy said, "Do you want to talk about what happened to you?"

"Do you mean how I was raped?"

"Yes!"

Kate looked at Mandy's face with a smile and replied, "Why not?" Kate told Mandy how she was raped by three guys. Mandy was so upset with the story and said, "That is horrible." Kate looked at her eyes with a smile and said, "I've got a plan for them."

"Do you mean the three men that raped you?" she asked.

"No, for all the men that I can get hold of," Kate replied.

"What do you mean by all the men you can get hold of? Do you want to turn yourself into prostitute?"

Kate looked at Mandy's face with a smile and replied, "What do you think I'm doing when I try to change my image?"

Mandy looked at Kate and shook her head left and right. "I know that you're up to something."

"Yes of course," Kate replied. Kate held Mandy's hand and said, "Follow me." They both went to the bedroom, where Kate showed Mandy all her collections.

"What are you going to do with all these?" Mandy asked.

Kate laughed and replied, "I will deal with them one by one."

"How?" Mandy asked.

In an anxious mood, Kate moved toward the living room with the collections of pictures of married celebrities in her hand. Mandy followed her and continued asking her what she was going to do with all the pictures. Kate sat down in the living room. Mandy looked at her eyes and said, "I still need a clear explanation about all these pictures."

Kate laughed and replied, "What do you think I changed my image for?" She went to the bedroom and brought some of her pictures she took at university and also before she had plastic surgery. Stretching her hand toward Mandy she said, "Take and look," with a harsh voice. Mandy looked at her face and took the pictures from her. Mandy glanced at the pictures, and she looked at Kate again and again. Mandy could see that there were big differences before Kate underwent her surgery.

"Why do you have to change your appearance?" she said.

"To carry out my plan," Kate replied.

"Why couldn't you tell me that you had a plan before I followed you to the plastic surgery?" Mandy asked.

Kate burst into laughter. .

"What's funny about this?" Mandy asked.

"Is it my fault or do you like what you see?" Kate replied.

Mandy looked at her face a smile and said, "You are a bad girl, you know." They both burst out laughing for about two minutes.

"Now tell me, how are you going to carry out this plan?" Mandy asked.

Kate looked at her eyes with a smile and replied, "I have achieved my first objective."

"What do you mean by that?" Mandy asked.

With a smile Kate replied, "To transform myself into a celebrity image and I am pleased with my image now."

"Then what next?" Mandy asked.

"To get myself a sophisticated surveillance camera," she replied.

Mandy shook her head left and right and said, "All these involve lots of money."

"That is why I am doing two jobs" Kate replied with a smile.

"Are you sure what you are doing is the right thing?" Mandy said.

Kate looked at her face and paused for some seconds and replied, "I have thought about it every day of my life since I was raped by Ian, Martin and Johnson. I also ask myself a question, did I deserve this? But something in my mind, is telling me that I should teach them a lesson."

Mandy intervened with a harsh voice, "Teach them a lesson! I do not think so. These are not the pictures of Ian, Martin and Johnson that raped you."

Kate looked at her with a smile and replied with a cool voice, "You are right! But men have to pay the price of what those three bastards did to me."

Mandy was silent and continued to look at Kate's eyes. Kate realised what Mandy was doing and said, "Have you forgiven your former boyfriend that raped you?"

"Yes of course," Mandy replied.

"That means you let him get away with it?"

"No, I cannot fight for myself as you're trying to do. I leave everything in the hands of God to fight for me."

Kate burst into laughter. "God!!"

"Our God is a patient God that forgives every soul when you confess your sins to him. That is the reason why you should allow him to fight for you," Mandy said.

"If every woman was like you, who aren't bothered who rapes them, what do you think the world would look like?"

"I don't know," Mandy replied.

"The world would be in a mess," Kate said.

Mandy shook her head left and right and said, "Maybe you are right! But not everybody are so stubborn as you are, Mandy said.

Kate smiled and said, "Believe me, I learned to be strong after I was raped, that is why I haven't had a boyfriend since then."

Mandy laughed and replied, "Life is too short, my dear, you need to move on or do you think because someone dies in the water, because of that you are not going to drink water anymore?" "No Mandy, if I have a boyfriend, he might be a good man who will change me for good, not to think about revenge any more. Or he might be a bad one that might rape me again, adding suffering to my suffering."

"I can see that you are determined to punish men," Mandy replied.

With a smile Kate nodded her head up and down to say yes.

"Have you ever thought about the downside of your plan?" Mandy asked.

"Yes of course," she replied. "At least if I try ten men, if nine fail one will succeed.

Are you going to lend me money to buy the sophisticated surveillance camera to carry out my revenge operation?" Kate asked .

Mandy burst into laughter.

"What is so funny about this?" Kate asked.

"Nothing, my dear, it would be stupid for me to lend you money to buy instruments to destroy the lives of people like me."

"Anyway, I do not need your money to carry out my plan."

"Thank you for asking," Mandy replied.

"Please could we stop discussing men and try to enjoy our weekend," Kate said.

"Yes, of course," Mandy replied. By this time it was nearly 3 o'clock, and Mandy lay on the sofa chair while Kate was trying to tidy up the house.

After Kate finished she came to the living room and sat down with Mandy to watch television. Not more than two minutes later the bell rang. Kate looked at Mandy's face and asked, "Are you expecting someone?"

"No Kate! Moreover, nobody knows that I'm spending the weekend with you." Kate stood up to open the door. Mandy stood up to know who was at the door.

It was a man and a woman, Jehovah's Witnesses, praising the words of God. As the man went to open his mouth to talk, Kate realised that they were Jehovah's Witnesses. With a polite manner, Kate said, "I'm not interested," and shut the door. Where Mandy was standing she could see them, as a result she didn't bother to ask. When they sat down Mandy looked at Kate's face and smiled.

"What have I done?" Kate asked.

"Nothing!" Mandy replied. She kept on smiling. Kate knew that she wanted to say something.

"Spill it out what's on your mind," she said.

"You could have let them preach for you, to see whether you could change your mind," Mandy said.

Kate laughed and said, "Your own preaching is more than their preaching, so I do not need your preaching, or their preaching anymore."

"I know that one day you will change your mind," Mandy said.

"Let us wait for that day, madam preacher," Kate replied with a deep, funny voice.

Kate and Mandy promised each other to be silent about Kate's revenge and decided to enjoy their weekend. They watched movies and prepared nice food for themselves to eat. On Sunday evening at about six o'clock, Mandy left Kate's to go to her flat to prepare for the next working day. When Mandy got to her flat she lay on her bed thinking about what Kate was planning to do, and how she could stop her.

But she did not want to tell anybody because she did not want to jeopardise her relationship with Kate. Throughout that month Kate tried to complete all her plastic surgery and worked hard to buy the materials she needed to use to carry out her plan. The only setback was that any time Katie worked with Mandy, Mandy would try everything to discourage her from her revenge.

One day Kate was upset with Mandy about the revenge matter because she kept reminding her every day and she decided not to talk to Mandy anymore. When Mandy realised what she had done she apologised, and they both continued their friendship again. Mandy realised that nobody could stop Kate, so she decided to support Kate with some advice. Kate worked hard for two months to save enough for her first trip to carry out her first plan.

She collected information from magazines, internet or anywhere she thought she could get hold of information about the first person she wanted to deal with. Kate realised that the first celebrity she wanted to deal with was going to film in New Zealand in about two weeks time. She applied for leave from her work place. She lied that her mother was seriously sick in the countryside and she was going to take care of her. Kate's leave was quickly approved by her manager because she had lied.

Kate travelled to New Zealand to investigate the hotel the first celebrity she was going to deal with would stay when he arrived in New Zealand for filming. After she found the hotel she then booked in that morning. The hotel manager was unable to refuse Kate's booking because her appearance was so glamorous that she looked like a multi-millionaire lady and he gave her special treatment. Before Kate left home for her journey she had ordered a wicked sex DVD from the internet. She kept it from Mandy , but she had watched the film several times. Immediately Kate checked in, she placed her mini camera in position near the bed. The camera was to record all the action she might perform with any man in the bed.

After fixing all the gadgets, she took her shower and dressed for action. Kate wore her best clothes for day one of her operation, and if any men saw her they wouldn't be able to resist. She looked at herself several times in the mirror and saw that she was looking good. She then walked down to the foyer to get more information from the manager about the married celebrity that had previously stayed in that hotel.

When the hotel manager saw her he couldn't resist, he moved towards her and asked, "How can I help you madam?"

"I just need some fresh air," Kate replied with a wicked smile.

The manager pointed toward the guest rest room and said, "There is the guest rest room if you don't mind, madam!"

"Thank you very much for your help," she replied.

Kate entered the guest room and sat down in the corner with the intention that the hotel manager would come and ask her what she would like to drink. There was a young couple sitting in the rest room, relaxing with a bottle of wine on their table. Immediately Kate walked in, the man started looking at Kate, amazed. Kate saw him and smiled at him while his wife wasn't looking.

But when his wife realised that he was looking at Kate all the time and not paying attention to her, she said to her husband they should go to their room. Kate was left in the guest room alone, reading a magazine that was on the table in front of her. About five minutes later the manager walked in and said, "I am sorry, madam, for leaving you for so long."

As the manager wanted to continue talking, Kate intervened, "That is alright. I know that you are busy at the moment preparing for your big guest who is coming."

"How do you know, madam, that we are having a visitor today?" he asked.

"I heard it from the couple that just left the room a few minutes ago," Kate replied.

"I'm very pleased that you understand, madam." Kate replied with thanks and smiling. "Now what can I offer you madam?"

Orange juice please," Kate replied with a cool voice.

"What about wine or spirits?"

Kate smiled and said, "I do not drink alcohol."

"But wine is not too bad," the manager said with a smile.

"Alright, a glass of red wine would be better," Kate replied. The manager called the bar man to bring a glass of red wine, and within two minutes the wine was in front of Kate. Kate looked at the barman and said, "That was very quick."

The barman smiled and the manager intervened with a smile, "It's our duty to serve our customers quickly in order to meet their demands."

"That is very sweet of you," Kate replied with a cool voice.

Kate looked at the manager's eyes and asked, "Are you not drinking anything?"

"No madam, I'm on duty at the moment."

"If you are on duty, you are not allowed to drink?" she asked.

We have a zero alcohol policy," the manager replied.

Kate was about to ask another question, when one of

the hotel receptionists rushed in and said to the manager that their visitor had arrived.

"Please madam, excuse me," the manager said.

"With all pleasure," Kate replied. As the manager left, Kate thought in her mind, "This is my moment." She went to the ladies toilet and topped up her make-up to prepare her for the moment.

She came out glamorously and moved slowly to the foyer and continued   chatting with one of the hotel staff. As Jackson was led into the hotel foyer by the hotel manager he glanced through the foyer, and amazingly his eyes and Kate's eyes made contact; and immediately Jackson was attracted to her.

In his look, Kate could see that she had won his soul. Jackson was taken to his room by the manager while cool champagne was on the table waiting for him to cool his mind down after the long journey. Kate went to her room, which happened to be on the same floor as Jackson's. After Jackson had finished his shower he rang the hotel manager and asked for the lady he had seen in the foyer when he was coming in.

The hotel manager quickly recognised that it was Kate. "She is on the same floor as you," the hotel manager replied. Jackson wrote a few lines of a letter and sealed the envelope and asked, "Could you please deliver this envelope to her?"

"Yes, of course," the hotel manager replied. He went to Kate's room and knocked on the door.

Kate opened the door gently. "I've got a message for you, madam," the manager said, and he stretched out his hand to give the envelope to Kate reluctantly.

"Where did the message come from?" Kate asked.

"The message is from our visitor," replied the manager.

"Do you mean Jackson?" Kate asked.

"Yes," the hotel manager replied.

"Thank you very much," Kate said, and she took the envelope from his hand. She closed the door and jumped onto her bed with laughter and joy. "I will teach them a lesson," she said repeatedly, while kissing the envelope as she was opening it.

Inside the envelope there was a letter saying, "If you don't mind, could you have dinner with me tonight''? Kate jumped up and down on her bed with the words, "yes of course, yes of course." Kate was full of joy at that moment. But within a minute she realised that the media would be following Jackson around and she might be a victim of publicity. She rang for the attention of the hotel manager to know about the media policy in the hotel.

"We do not allow the media into the hotel unless their attention is asked for, and there are procedures they need to follow according to the hotel policy. Why do you need to ask for the media policy madam?" the hotel manager asked.

"He asked me to have dinner with him tonight," Kate replied with a smile.

"Do you mean Jackson?" the hotel manager asked.

"Yes," Kate replied with a smile on her face.

"Madam, do not worry about Jackson, there are special dining rooms all our celebrities normally use."

"Do you mean that there is a special dining room designed for them?" she asked.

"Yes," the hotel manager replied. As he was about to close the door, Kate said, "Thank you very much."

"With all pleasure, madam," he replied.

Kate ordered champagne to celebrate her first move and hailed it as a success. As Kate was drinking the champagne, she moved around her room in the front of the mirror, acting how she was going to walk and talk to him at the dinner table.

She looked through her window to see what was going on outside the hotel. Kate was surprised as she saw lots of media surrounding the hotel just to get a shot of Jackson. Kate was angry that the hotel manager was lying to her. She sat down on her bed thinking what to do. She knew that if she appeared in the newspapers it would damage all her plans for revenge. Also the news would carry it and it would be embarrassing to her friend Mandy.

As Kate was thinking about the media, she fell asleep and she was dreaming. In her dream she saw that Mandy was marrying one of the guys who had raped her. She was so angry with Mandy in that dream and she confronted Martin, Mandy's husband, and told him that he was not going to get away with it. She woke up terrified about the dream and she picked up the phone and called Mandy and told her about the dream. Mandy told her not to worry about her, that she was not thinking of getting married now. Also, Kate told Mandy that she was having dinner with Jackson tonight. Mandy was surprised that Kate had got her way through to the married celebrity.

She told Kate to be very careful and that she could not wait to see her again. After the conversation with Mandy on the phone, Kate showered to get herself ready for the dinner. Kate wore one of her best dresses and she looked stunning. She was in two minds whether to cancel the dinner because of the media or to believe what the hotel manager had told her. Someone knocked on the door; Kate moved towards the door and opened it gently. She saw it was the hotel manager.

"Come in please, you have a query to answer," she said with a harsh voice.

The hotel manager entered and saw how stunning Kate was. He said, "Madam you look beautiful."

"Never mind how I look," Kate replied with a polite voice.

The hotel manger was shocked how Kate spoke to him. He said, "What have I done Madam?"

"Have you looked at the media that has surrounded this hotel?" "

Yes of course," the hotel manager replied with a smile.

"Why have you lied to me? I asked you about the media policy in the hotel."

"Madam, I'm not lying to you; moreover, I would not lie about our policy."

That's why you see that all these celebrities come back to us because we maintain their privacy."

Kate looked at the manager with a sideways look and said, "I'm very sorry to doubt you."

"That's alright, madam," he replied.

"Now why are you knocking my door?" Kate asked with a smile.

"It is time for dinner and Jackson wants you." Kate stood up and moved round the room and asked, "How do I look?"

"You look great," the hotel manager replied.

"Be my guest," Kate said. She put her hand across the hotel manager's hand and jammed the door.

Jackson was already in the celebrities' special dining room waiting for Kate.

Immediately he saw Kate coming with the hotel manager he stood up and offered her a seat. After Kate had sat down, he said with a cool voice, "You look beautiful."

"Thanks," she replied.

Kate had a lovely dinner with Jackson and was also impressed with the way he treated her. When they finished their dinner, Jackson said to Kate, "Please I cannot escort you to your room now because I need to make an urgent call."

"No problem, I will see you tomorrow," Kate replied.

As Kate was about to leave Jackson wrote a few words on a piece of paper, squeezed the paper and put it in Kate's hand, as he was saying goodbye. Kate did not open the paper until she got to her room. Immediately Kate entered the room, she jumped on her bed with joy that her plan was working. She was so delighted to have had dinner with Jackson. She poured champagne in a glass and walked around the room saying a toast to Jackson. Then she opened the paper in her hand to see what Jackson had written on it.

In the paper, he said "I will see you tonight at about quarter to midnight." Kate jumped on her bed again and again saying, "I will prepare for you." She put all her surveillance cameras in place to catch the action with Jackson in bed. She rushed to take her shower and put on her night gown. Kate ordered another bottle of champagne because the one that was on her table was nearly finished, and because she was so excited to have had dinner with Jackson. She said to the waitress, "Let the champagne chill in the ice."

Although Kate had tried to avoid alcohol since she was raped, she drank the champagne to cheer herself up because the plan was going accordingly. Kate saw that everything was in place, the champagne on ice on the table and the surveillance camera was okay. She sat down on the sofa to relax herself, but she fell asleep. When Jackson arrived at a quarter to twelve, Kate had dozed off. He knocked and there was no response. He wrote some words on a piece of paper and passed it inside through the bottom of the door. When Kate woke up it was one thirty in the morning. She was so annoyed that she started kicking the table in front of her with the words, "Fuck me."

After she calmed down, she saw a piece of white paper behind the door. She opened the paper. The words said, "I'm very, very sorry that you were absent when I called. Please try to call me in the morning through the hotel manager, your lovely Jackson." With anger, Kate squeezed the paper and put it in the bin. She switched off her surveillance equipment and went to bed with anger. In the morning, Kate woke up late. By the time she called the hotel manager to ask for Jackson, he was already on the site where he was about to film.

Kate was so sad that the hotel manager noticed that something was wrong with her. Kate had only booked in for a week in the hotel, which meant every day she lost, meant a lots to her. Jackson also worried about Kate being absent when he called to her room. In the afternoon, he called the hotel to talk to the hotel manager who told him the situation. He saw Kate in the morning, and she wasn't impressed. "Did she tell you what the matter with her was?" Jackson asked.

"No, just asked about you," the hotel manager replied.

"Could you tell her that I will see her in the evening?" he asked.

"Yes, of course," the hotel manager replied.

Immediately Jackson dropped the telephone, the hotel manager went and delivered the massage to Kate. Kate was so excited about the message that she jumped up and down on her bed. Kate had targeted Jackson because he was a married celebrity. Kate believed she could demand a huge amount of money from Jackson after recording her affair with him. But what she didn't realise was that Jackson's lawyer had served Jackson's wife divorce papers before Jackson left home to go to New Zealand.

Some of the papers had been carrying the rumours

about their marriage, which Kate had failed to spot. Also, when Jackson had dinner with Kate, in his mind he was thinking that this maybe was another opportunity for him to fall in love again. Although Kate wasn't thinking of love she was thinking of how to revenge the rape Ian, Martin and Johnson had carried out at University.

Kate did thorough research about the married celebrities she was going to deal with before she went to New Zealand. Jackson was 'number six' as she named him, but she grabbed the opportunity to deal with Jackson when she heard that he was going to film in New Zealand. In the evening when Jackson returned from the filming site, he sent the hotel manager to ask Kate to have dinner with him.

Kate quickly accepted the offer with joy but told the hotel manager that she would be there after she had finished taking her bath. When the hotel manager delivered the message to Jackson that Kate was on her way, Jackson was delighted. Jackson had confidence in the hotel manager because he had been using the hotel for some time and the hotel was one of the best for maintaining the privacy of celebrities.

He always recommended the hotel to some of his friends in Hollywood whenever they came to New Zealand for filming. Jackson was waiting for Kate in the dining room, but Kate had lied to the hotel manager about taking her bath. What she wanted to do was to buy time in order to set up her surveillance camera in case Jackson came home with her. After she finished setting up the surveillance camera she went to the dining room to meet Jackson.

"You are so beautiful," Jackson said to Kate.

"Thank you very much," Kate replied.

"What's kept you so long? I thought you were not coming."

"No, how can I lie to you? If I didn't want to come, I would say to the hotel manager to give you my message."

"Thank you for honouring my invitation for a second dinner," Jackson said with a smile.

"You are too sweet," Kate replied with a cool voice.

As they were eating, Jackson said, "Pardon me for asking you this question because I do not want to upset you, that is why I failed to ask you during our first dinner."

"Yes, of course you are free to ask anything," Kate said.

"What are you doing in New Zealand?"

Kate stopped eating and looked at Jackson's eyes with a smile. She replied, "I am here for a holiday." Jackson smiled and continued eating then Kate stretched her head across the table towards Jackson and said in a funny voice, "I don't need to ask you what you are doing in New Zealand because I already know that you are filming."

Jackson laughed. "You are too funny," he said.

After they had finished dinner, Kate was expecting Jackson to escort her to her room, but Jackson insisted that they should go to his room. Kate agreed because she did not want to act suspiciously, or for Jackson to know about her plan. Kate and Jackson enjoyed themselves throughout the night. Although it was long time since Kate had had sex with a man, she really enjoyed having sex with Jackson.

In Jackson's mind, Kate was a decent lady. This prompted him to be determined to have a strong relationship with her. In the morning, Kate woke Jackson up and said she was leaving after she had dressed . Jackson promised to see her in the evening.

As Kate opened the door and was about to leave, she looked back and said to Jackson who was still in bed, "That was nice." Jackson smiled and replied, "Thank you. Bye."

In Kate's room, she was worried about wasting her money coming to New Zealand if her plan did not work. She managed to take her shower and switched off the surveillance camera.

As she lay on her bed thinking what to do next, the hotel manager knocked on the door. Kate quickly opened the door because she thought it was Jackson.

"Good morning Madam," the hotel manager said.

"What can I do for you?" Kate replied.

"Can I come in?" he said.

"Yes of course," Kate replied.

The hotel manager came in and said, "Madam I've come to discuss how to refund your booking money to you."

When Kate had left Jackson's room, Jackson had called the hotel manager to return the money Kate had paid for the hotel.

"What do you mean by that?" Kate asked.

"Jackson wanted to pay for your stay here," the manager said. Kate was shocked and speechless. Then the hotel manager asked, "Do you want it in cheque or cash?"

"A cheque," Kate replied.

"I will go and talk to the management team about the refund, and then I will get back to you."

"Thank you very much," Kate replied.

When the hotel manager left Kate's room she started dancing around the room filled with joy.

An hour later the hotel manager came with a cheque and Kate was delighted. As the hotel manager was about to go, he said to Kate, "Are you going to spend another week here?".

"Do you mean Jackson is going to pay?" Kate replied.

The hotel manager looked at Kate's eyes with a big smile on his face. "You're not going to paid for the services," he said, and closed the door.

Kate threw the cheque in the air and danced around the room with joy.

In the afternoon Kate quickly rushed to pay the cheque into her account and did some shopping. Although she hadn't lost any money, she was still determined to record her action in bed with Jackson. Unfortunately, any time she set up her surveillance camera and expected Jackson to visit her, he did not turn up. Instead he would send a message for Kate to meet him in the dining room or his room. Kate was unable to turn down Jackson's requests because she could see he was not doing it purposefully. Also he filmed late and was so tired and he had to rest before he woke up early again. Kate put all these things to consideration, and decided not to force him to come to her room. Also, the way Jackson treated Kate was special, and she began to doubt in her mind whether she could settle down with a man. In her mind she believed that Jackson was not the right person because he was married and she just wanted to use him for money.

On the last night, which was Friday night, Kate wanted to leave the hotel . She sat on her bed recording herself, talking about her date with Jackson and how she had really enjoyed herself. Someone knocked on the door and Kate thought maybe it was the hotel manager or one of the hotel staff. She rushed to open the door and left the camera on. As she opened the door, she saw Jackson and she was shocked. "Why have you finished early?" she asked.

"Can I come in?" Jackson asked.

"Yes, of course," she replied.

Jackson came in and gave Kate a nice kiss and Kate responded by smiling.

"You are beautiful," Jackson said.

"Thank you my darling," she replied.

"What do you want to drink?" Kate asked.

"Champagne with ice would be very nice," he replied.

Kate called for champagne and ice from the bar. As they were waiting for the drink, Kate said, "I would like to use this opportunity to thank you for paying for my stay. Not only that, you gave me money to buy anything I want, what could I say other than to thank you?"

Jackson was impressed that Kate realised what he had done for her. He smiled and said, "Come here," Kate cuddled him and kissed him with emotional love.

As they were kissing each other, the hotel manager knocked on the door. Kate opened the door with a smile and the hotel manager said, "Here is champagne, Madam," in a funny voice.

"Thank you very much," Kate replied. As the hotel manager was about to leave, Kate said, "I will definitely come back again because of the service you have given me."

"Thank you, Madam," the hotel manager replied and closed the door.

Kate opened the drink and poured it into two glasses; she gave one to Jackson and took the other. She raised glass and said, "A toast to our relationship."

Jackson smiled and said, "You are very funny."

Kate moved towards him and cuddled him with kisses and said, "I've really enjoy my time with you."

"Thank you very much," Jackson replied with many kisses.

Kate took the glass from Jackson and placed it on the table with her own glass as she held Jackson's hand and drew him to the bed with kisses and cuddles. Jackson also responded with dozens of kisses. The tension was so high that Kate rolled over Jackson on the bed and started undoing his buttons and zip. There was lots of romance and kisses before they made love to each other that day. Kate went to extra lengths to show Jackson what she was capable of in bed. Jackson enjoyed making love to Kate, not because she looked beautiful, but she was also good in bed.

In the morning Jackson woke up early to go to his room, but Kate relaxed because she knew that day was the last day in the hotel. Meanwhile, in the morning before Jackson went filming, he issued a cheque for $50,000 to the hotel manager to pay into the hotel account and told he should re-issue the cheque to Kate before she left.

When Kate woke up, she went to shower and then packed her surveillance camera. She didn't even bother to look at her action with Jackson in the bed, which she had recorded, but she was pleased in her mind that that she performed well enough to blackmail Jackson.

However, she didn't know that Jackson was planning another thing for her. She was packing her luggage when someone knocked on the door. In a good mood, Kate rushed to open the door.

"Good morning, Madam," a lady from the management office, escorted by the hotel manager, said. Kate was too shocked to reply because she thought something might have happened to Jackson.

"Please Madam, don't be surprised. Nothing has happened," the lady said.

Kate placed her left palm into her chest and replied, "Come in. " The lady and the manager came in and sat down. Kate wasn't sure whether something was about to happen and she continued looking at them to hear the news. Then the lady said, "Management have given this cheque to the manager to give to you.

But it's our procedure that when the hotel issues a

cheque for more than $20,000 then the receiver has to sign some documents."

As she had mentioned thousands, Kate looked at her, surprised, and said, "What are you talking about?"

The lady looked at Kate's eyes and smiled. Kate faced the hotel manager and asked, "What is going on?"

The lady from the management office intervened. "Nothing has happened, Madam.

Mr Jackson said we should give you this cheque, which is why I came with the manager for you to sign the document that you have received the cheque."

"No, no, no, you are joking," Kate said with surprise.

"Madam, there is no way I could joke about $50,000," the lady replied. Kate was shocked – she sat down on the bed for about five minutes before she signed the document.

"Thank you Madam, we hope you will come back to us again," the lady said and left with the hotel manager.

Kate was speechless; she started to cry with emotion and started having doubts about her plan with Jackson.

In the afternoon before Kate left the hotel, she quickly went to the bank to pay the money into her account. The lady at the counter saw that the cheque was from one of their customers at the hotel. She contacted the hotel to ask whether they had issued a cheque for $50,000 to someone, before they allowed the cheque in. Meanwhile, before she reached the hotel, Jackson had phoned to ask whether she had left.

As Kate came in, the hotel manager delivered the message to her that Jackson had phoned. Kate went to her room. As she opened the door, the phone rang. It was Jackson on the phone. Kate was crying with the words, "Thank you very much," again and again. Jackson told her not to cry and wished her a safe journey home. He promised her that he would get in touch with her when she reached home.

"Thank you very, very much; I will not forget what you have done for me," Kate said.

After Kate finished talking with Jackson, she called the hotel manager to order a taxi to take her to the airport. Kate rang Mandy to tell her the time her flight was going to take off and also the time she would land at the airport. Meanwhile, Mandy was waiting for Kate at the airport in order to hear the outcome of her plan.

Inside the plane on the way home Kate was so delighted; not because she had succeeded in her plan alone but also because she felt like a woman because since she had been raped in the university, she had never slept with another man.

On arrival at Gatwick Airport, from a distance Mandy could notice the happiness on Kate's face.

"I can see happiness on your face, Kate," said Mandy.

With a smile Kate replied, "My journey was blessed."

As Mandy wanted to continue talking, Kate, intervened. "Did you bring your car or did you take the train?"

"Of course, the car is outside," Mandy replied. They both walked through the car park to Mandy's car. Mandy opened the boot and Kate put her bag inside.

Mandy started the car and drove out of the car park. "Now tell me about your journey," Mandy said.

Kate replied with a smile, "Everything went according to plan."

"Do you mean you got him?"

"Yes, of course," Kate replied.

Mandy shook her head left and right and said, "Men !! They are bastards. Did you record you and him in bed?"

"What do you think when I spent lots of money on buying equipment?

Though it was only one day I could record, it means a lot to me."

Mandy kept silent and concentrated on driving. Then Kate said, "Another thing happened along the way."

"What do you mean by that?" Mandy asked.

"I eventually fell in love with him," Kate said. Mandy laughed. "Love!" Mandy said with a funny voice and continued laughing.

"I'm very, very serious Mandy," replied Kate. When Mandy looked at Kate's face as she was talking, Mandy noticed that she was serious.

"What are you going to do about it now?" Mandy asked. Kate rested her head on the car seat and tears fell from her eyes. Mandy parked the car and cuddled her and told her not to cry. When Kate regained herself, Mandy started the car and drove on.

"He treated me like a queen," Kate said.

"Do you mean Jackson?"

"Yes!"

"Did you get his contact number?" Mandy asked.

"No, he would not give his number to anybody in case of security reasons," Kate replied.

"But how would you contact him then?"

"He took my mobile number," Kate replied.

"I hate to tell you this," Mandy said.

"What, what?" Kate replied with a harsh voice.

"The day you travelled to New Zealand it was in the news that Jackson had filed divorce papers against his wife."

"No, you are lying, Mandy."

"I'm not lying. It was also in the newspapers I kept at home."

Kate was so confused about the whole situation, and

whether to travel back to New Zealand to meet Jackson or continue her plan. Mandy's intention was to drive Kate to her own flat for her to have a little bit of rest before going to her flat. Because Kate was not happy about Jackson's divorce, she told Mandy to drive her to her own flat. Despite the amount of money Jackson gave to Kate, she was still in doubt whether to make more money through the tape she had recorded by sending it to Jackson. By hearing that Jackson was divorcing his wife, she knew that her plan was not going to work.

At Kate's flat, after she had finished showering, she told Mandy about her travelling and how she had bedded Mr Jackson. Mandy relaxed as Kate was telling her all about her travel experiences. After she had finished, Mandy asked, "Is he good in bed?" with a funny voice.

"Yes, he is perfect," Kate answered with a smile

"Does he good than you in bed?"

"Do you mean in action?" Kate replied.

"Yes! I tried to perform more than him, but he is so strong and energetic."

Mandy put her left hand on her jaw and lay her elbow on the dining table with a smile. She said, "I cannot blame you; it's a long time since you have had sex."

Kate laughed and replied, "I really tried my possible best to perform more than him on the last day I had sex with him because I was recording the action.

But I couldn't, he was too strong for me. "

"Did you enjoy having sex with him?" Mandy asked.

Kate looked at Mandy's eyes with emotional love and replied, "He is the type of guy I would go for. His romance, kissing and physical sex were perfect. If I had my chance in the future, I would marry him."

Mandy took a deep breath and shook her head up and down and said, "Thank God that I've started to hear positive things coming out from your mouth. What do you mean by that? You have never spoken about marriage before, now I can hear it from your mouth."

With a smile, Kate replied, "The journey made me think about many things I could only dream of."

"Now, could we watch the tape you have recorded?" Mandy asked. Kate looked at Mandy's face with a smile and replied "No," shaking her head left and right.

Mandy was surprised that Kate didn't want to show the tape to her. "But you promised to show the tape when you arrived," Mandy said.

"I've changed my mind, I don't want to show the tape to anybody. I will destroy the tape."

"How could you destroy the tape when you wanted to use it to make money?"

Kate smiled and replied, "I have already got the money."

"What do you mean by that?" Mandy asked.

"He paid for my week's stay in the expensive hotel and also gave me $50,000."

"What!" Mandy shouted with surprise. "Are you joking Kate?"

"No, I'm not." Kate opened her bag and showed Mandy the receipt she had used to pay the money into her account.

When Mandy saw the receipt she was speechless and Kate looked at her eyes and said, "Don't you see how lucky I am?"

"Yes, I do," Mandy replied. Now, what are you going to do next?"

"I need to reduce my working hours and plan for my next adventure," Kate replied with a funny voice.

"Lucky you, lady," Mandy said.

After they prepared something to eat, Kate said,

"I'm going to leave my supermarket job this week."

"Why do you want to do that?" Mandy asked.

Kate smiled and said, "I need to have time for myself with the little money I've got."

"That is very sensible," Mandy replied. But the problem is that when nothing comes in and you are spending the money, you will finish the money."

"Thank you for your good advice," Kate said. "Before the money is finished I will think of something else to do."

As Kate and Mandy was talking, Kate's phone rang.

Kate felt reluctant to answer the call, she looked at Mandy , and Mandy made a sign that she should answer the call. Kate picked up her mobile and said, "Hello!" It was Kate's manager at work that had called. She asked whether she would come to work on Monday. Kate quickly replied, "No!"

"Why?" she asked.

"Something came up on the way, I need some time for myself," Kate replied. "I think it's nothing too serious."

"No!"

"But I need to have time for myself," Kate replied.

"Good luck with anything you do," said the manager.

"Thanks," Kate replied.

Mandy looked at Kate's eyes and said, "Money is talking."

Kate laughed and replied, "I wish I had enough!"

By this time, it was getting late and Mandy said, "I need to go home and will see you tomorrow."

"Thank you for everything," Kate said. She escorted Mandy to her car and cuddled her and said, "Goodbye, see you tomorrow." As Kate returned to her flat the phone rang, and before she could pick it up , it stopped ringing. Kate tried to trace the call but the number was withheld. Kate brought out the tape she had recorded when she was in bed with Jackson in the hotel.

As she was trying to fix the equipment with her television to watch the tape, her phone rang. Kate looked at the table clock and picked up the phone.

"Hello, good evening, Kate speaking, how can I help you?" she said.

Jackson laughed and replied on the phone that she sounded sweet. When Kate realised that it was Jackson's voice she was so pleased. "Where are you calling from?" she asked.

"Why do you ask?" he replied.

"Because it is late," Kate said.

"Is it too late for me to call you?" Jackson asked with a funny voice.

"No, no," said Kate.

"I just want to know that you arrived home safely," he said.

"Thank you very much. You are a genius," Kate said.

"It is my duty to protect you as much as I can," replied Jackson.

"That is very sweet of you," Kate said. As she was talking to Jackson on the mobile, she fixed the recorder to the television to rewind the tape. She also thanked Jackson for his generosity when she was in New Zealand.

"I really enjoyed the time you spent with you," Jackson replied. He ended the conversation by saying, "I love you, baby."

Kate was so happy to talk to Jackson and after he had hung up, Kate quickly rang Mandy to tell her she had just finished talking to Jackson on the phone.

"What did he say?" Mandy asked.

"Nothing," Kate replied. "He just wanted to know whether I arrived home safely." "That's very sweet of him," Mandy said.

"He is a sweet guy," Kate replied.

"Did he say that he would be getting in touch?"

"Yes, of course," Kate replied.

"Lucky you," Mandy said with a funny deep voice.

Kate laughed and said, "I'm just watching our performance on the bed." Before Kate finished talking, Mandy shouted in surprise, "Is it good?"

Kate laughed and replied with a deep funny voice, "It is perfect."

"Are you going to show me this tape?" Mandy asked.

"No, it's only me who can watch it," Kate replied.

"It is not fair for only you to watch it , because that was not the plan before you travelled."

"I'm very sorry Mandy; you need to wait for the second show."

"What do you mean by that?" Mandy asked.

"I have told you what I'm going to do to any man who comes across me."

"Do you mean you are still going to continue with your plan?" Mandy asked.

"Yes, of course," she replied.

Mandy took a long breath and said with a sad voice, "But you said you fell in love with Jackson. Why can't you stay with him? I am sure he loves you also, that is why he phoned to make sure you'd reached home safely."

Kate laughed. "What are you laughing about?" Mandy asked.

"Please, I don't want to discuss this anymore, I have told you my plan and my plan still remains the same," Kate replied.

"After all that he has done for you, can't you realise that?" Mandy asked.

"Thank you Madam Preacher, I am tired, let me

have some rest, I will talk to you tomorrow," Kate said.

Kate ended the conversation and went to bed.

In the morning, after she had brushed her teeth and prepared a cup of tea, she brought her collections out to look at who would be the next celebrity she needed to deal with. Kate knew that Jackson was serious about their relationship, and Kate loved him also. \She just wanted to gamble with two more celebrities before she could be serious with Jackson.

But how to meet them became difficult for Kate. She then realised that the Cannes Film Festival was coming up in France in May, and that would be another opportunity for her to meet the celebrities. She tried to get information about where her next targeted celebrity was going to stay, but she couldn't get the information. She thought if she discussed it with Jackson, he might suspect her and start asking her questions why she wanted to know about Robert.

Although Kate didn't know, Robert was Jackson's best friend. She'd just picked him randomly as the next celebrity to deal with. As Kate was battling in her mind who to get information from, Robert went to the Cannes festival.

Mandy rang. Kate picked up the phone to say hello to Mandy. As they were about to finish their early morning gossip," Kate said to Mandy, "I have selected my second client."

Mandy laughed and replied, "What do you mean by second client?"

"I have told you that I don't want to be discussing these plans with you again, because I have already told you what I'm planning to do to all these men.

The only problem I'm facing at this moment is how I'm going to get information about him," Kate said.

"I cannot help you because I don't know your next client," Mandy replied with a funny voice.

Kate laughed. "That is very funny, Mandy, she said. "Anyway, my next client is Robert."

"You know his wife is also popular?" Mandy said.

"That is lovely," Kate replied. "That's what makes him suitable for my next target." Mandy laughed. "You have known him, how do you think I can get information about him?" Kate asked.

"You are asking the wrong person," Mandy replied.

"Why can't you get the information from Jackson? He will be the right person to talk to," Mandy said.

Kate took a deep breath and replied, "I have thought about it, but the problem is that I am not too sure whether I am going to end up having a good relationship with him because I still love him despite my plan."

"I don't think that is the matter," Mandy said.

What if he has doubts in his mind about me by asking him?"

"You will tell him that you are doing some project about the Hollywood stars," said Mandy.

"That is it, Mandy, you are brilliant," Kate replied. "Anytime he calls again, I will ask him."

"But how are you going to meet Robert?" Mandy asked.

"The Cannes festival in France is just around the corner and I know that he is going there," Kate replied.

"Good luck," Mandy said.

"I need it," Kate replied and put down the phone.

After Kate and Mandy's conversation, Kate wasn't sure whether to ask Jackson about Robert. She really considered not blowing her chances with Jackson, because of what he had done for her. Also, she knew that Jackson loved her and to ask him about another man seemed inappropriate.

Kate was in a dilemma, with a troubled mind about the Robert issue, so she decided not to ask Jackson.

Throughout that week Jackson did not call Kate because he was so busy filming. He came home late and he didn't want to disturb Kate at all when she was in bed. Kate was also wondering what had really happened when Jackson did not call. Maybe he had changed his mind about her and wanted to end the relationship. Kate tried to be normal whenever she was with her friend, Mandy, because she didn't want Mandy to know that Jackson hadn't called her. That week passed. Kate tried hard to keep herself going, but on Tuesday of the following week, Mandy and Kate were going shopping, and Mandy noticed that Kate was not as cheerful as she usually was.

"What is the matter, Kate?" she asked.

"Nothing," Kate replied.

"It doesn't seem to me that nothing's wrong," Mandy said. As Kate went to open her mouth, she burst in tears. Mandy cuddled her. "Do not cry," she said. Mandy gave Kate a tissue from her bag to clean her face and Kate burst into laughter as she cleaned her face. When Mandy saw Kate regain herself, she asked her what was the matter. Kate took a deep breath and replied, "Jackson hasn't called throughout the last week."

Mandy burst into laughter and Kate was a little bit upset. "What is funny about this?" she asked. Instead of replying, Mandy continued to laugh. When Kate saw that Mandy wasn't bothered about whether she was upset or not, she joined her and they both continued to laugh again and again. Kate looked at Mandy's face as she was laughing, and tears started to fall from Mandy's eyes.

After they had finished laughing, Mandy said, "Do you think he has dumped you?"

"I don't know," Kate replied.

Mandy looked at Kate's face and started to laugh

whenever she asked Kate the question. Kate was upset and said, "I'm not going to answer any of your questions again unless you stop laughing." Then Mandy stopped laughing and they both discussed Mr Jackson's attitude in not calling Kate.

After they finished shopping, on their way home, Kate's mobile rang. She answered the phone, hoping that it might be Mr Jackson. "Sorry, it is the wrong number," the man on the other end said. Mandy looked at Kate's eyes and asked who it was. "It was a wrong number," Kate replied.

Then Mandy smiled. "Why are you smiling?" Kate asked. Instead of Mandy replying, she burst into laughter. Kate looked at her and shook her head left and right and said, "You are not serious at all."

"Yes, I know," Mandy replied. Kate and Mandy went to Kate's flat and had a good day. In the evening, Mandy left Kate to go to her own flat.

Kate was totally wrecked and disappointed by Jackson not calling her. She even forgot her plans to punish married celebrities and started to doubt her chances of having a long term relationship with Jackson. Kate was unable to sleep because of the matter on her mind. She sat in the living room watching television and playing some love songs. By quarter to four (3.45 am), Kate fell asleep on her sofa. When it was exactly 5.00am, her phone rang. She managed to pick up the phone and said, "Hello," with her eyes heavily closed.

Surprise, surprise, it was Jackson. Kate jumped up when she heard his voice. "Why did you not call me throughout last week?" she said with anger.

"I'm very sorry," Jackson replied. "As you know, before you left New Zealand we were just starting filming and now we are in the middle of the project and we are busy all the time. That is why I did not have the time to call you. Also I came in too late at night and I did not want to disturb you when you were sleeping."

Kate laughed and replied, "Did I complain that you were disturbing me? You could have tried first and let me complain before any excuses."

"I'm very sorry," Jackson replied.

"I'm very, very upset that you did not call me for a whole week," Kate said.

"I'm very sorry, babe," Jackson replied.

"I forgive you this time and don't let it happen again," Kate said with a smile on her face.

"Yes Madam," Jackson replied with a funny voice.

"I like that," Kate said with a smile. Now, how are you?"

"I'm fine," Jackson replied.

"I hope you are not looking at another lady's face," Kate said in a funny voice.

"No! I do not have time for that because I have got what I want," Jackson replied.

"What do you mean by that?" she asked.

"I have got you and don't need to look around again."

Kate laughed and replied, "That is very sweet of you. Now you said that you're busy filming, are you not going to the Cannes Film Festival in France?"

"No, I will not be able to go this year," Jackson replied. "I'm going to miss most of my friends that are going."

"Do you want to go?" Jackson asked.

"I'm not a Hollywood star, nobody's going to recognise me there," Kate replied. "However, if I want to go, I cannot avoid the travelling and accommodation expenses." Jackson took a deep breath and said, "Go and have fun, I will send a ticket to you and also book the hotel you're going to stay in."

"Are you serious?" Kate asked with surprise in her

voice.

"If that is what you want, I have to do it for you," Jackson replied.

Kate started to scream on the phone with the words, "You are a darling, you're a darling."

As she wanted to end the conversation, Jackson said, "Before you go, I will call some of my friends who can look after you."

Kate thanked Jackson so much and started to cry for joy on the phone. Jackson told her not to cry and she should go back to bed and relax . Jackson kissed her on the phone and said goodbye.

Kate was emotionally high and started to cry after Jackson hung up the phone. After she regained herself she was overjoyed that Jackson hadn't dumped her. Jackson had talked to Kate on the phone for almost an hour before he hung up the phone. Kate was delighted about the conversation, she couldn't keep it to herself. She rang Mandy at half past six in the morning and told her the good news. Mandy was deeply asleep and couldn't listen to Kate's conversation.

Although she picked up the phone and pretended that she was listening, half of Kate's conversation missed her ears. Kate hadn't realised that Mandy was not listening to her conversation properly, because she was full of joy about what Jackson had promised her. She was just talking and laughing on the phone. When she was expecting a reply, Mandy did not respond. Then she realised that Mandy wasn't listening to her. She then ended the conversation and said, "I will see you later in the morning after breakfast." Mandy realised that Kate had called her early in the morning, but she wasn't sure what to discuss with her. She decided to call Kate and find out what they had been talking about. She called Kate's house number and the line was engaged. She then tried her mobile number.

The mobile was switched off. Mandy decided to wait for some minutes before she decided to try Kate's number again.

However, Kate was talking to her parents in the countryside. Her parents asked her about Paulina. Kate told them that she hadn't seen her for a long time because she had lost her number when she moved home. Kate just briefed her parents on how life was going in the City and that she was doing well. But she kept her relationship with Jackson a secret from her parents simply because she was not sure whether she wanted a commitment or not. Despite the fact that she liked Jackson, it was still in the back of her mind that she should punish men for what they had done to her. Whenever Kate remembered the rape she forgot about Jackson entirely and started thinking about revenge. But any time she was in a good mood, she talked about Jackson all the time. Immediately after Kate had finished talking to her parents, Mandy called her. Kate picked up the phone and Mandy said, "I have been ringing your number but the line was engaged.

Who were you talking to?"

I was talking to my parents," Kate replied.

"You were talking to me this morning on the phone; I cannot remember what we were talking about."

Kate breathed in and replied, "I know that you were not listening to the conversation because you were sleeping."

"Has that offended you?" Mandy asked.

"Not at all!" Kate replied. "The only thing is that it took me some time before I realised that you were not listening."

"I'm very sorry about that," Mandy replied. "Now tell me, what were you calling me for in the early morning like that?"

"I just wanted to tell you that Jackson phoned me

this morning and when I was finished with him I decided to share the good news with you."

"Did you ask him about the information you need from him?"

"What do you mean Mandy?"

"Please do not pretend that you don't know what I'm talking about," Mandy said.

Kate smiled and replied, "Yes, of course I know what you are talking about. But for your information, Jackson said that he is so busy filming, he is not going to the Cannes Film Festival and he wants me to go and have fun. He even promised to send travel tickets and money that I'm going to spend for me to enjoy myself when I get there."

"Lucky you, for you to fulfil your dream," Mandy said.

"Is that all you are going to say?" Kate asked with a harsh voice.

"What do you want me to say? Do you want me to praise you that you are doing well? No, Kate! Can't you see how this guy loves you and you are still thinking of how to take revenge? If I was in your shoes, I would stop all this nonsense and concentrate on him. Who knows whether he will be your husband in the future?"

Kate was so upset about the way that Mandy was talking to her that she replied in a harsh voice, "Did I call you for a lecture this morning? Or did I tell you that I needed your advice?" Kate wanted to continue but Mandy intervened, "My friend I'm just telling you the right thing. If you like, you can accept it. If you don't like, you can reject it.

But when it's going to bounce back on you, the repercussions will be very great."

Kate could not take in all what Mandy was telling her and she put down the phone with her finger. Mandy tried to redial Kate's number but she refused to answer her call, but Mandy continued to redial the number with the intention that Kate would answer the phone. However, Kate ignored the phone when it was ringing without stopping. Kate planned in her mind to keep away from Mandy for some time. Kate was worried about Mandy's behaviour, she began to doubt in her mind whether she should have revealed her secret to Mandy . Although she decided to keep away from her, she could not avoid her because they saw each other at work. Mandy wasn't worried too much about Kate because she knew that she would come back.

Meanwhile, after Mandy finished talking with Kate, she wanted to go downstairs to the corner shop to buy milk. As Mandy stepped outside her flat, there was a handsome man standing opposite . Mandy pretended that she couldn't see the man and entered the shop. But the man followed Mandy and stood at the front corner of the shop, expecting to talk to her when she came out of the shop. Mandy picked up the milk from the open freezer and walked towards the shop assistant to pay for it. She looked back and saw the man standing outside the shop. Mandy knew that the man was waiting for her.

After she paid she decided to spend a little time in the shop by looking around. The man saw that Mandy didn't want to come out because of him. He walked in, went straight to Mandy and said, "Hi," with a smile on his face. Mandy could not resist, she looked at his face with a smile.

"I know that you don't want to come out because of me!" he said with a funny voice. Mandy looked at his eyes again with a smile and replied, "That is funny." She walked out of the shop and the man followed her. As they stepped out the man said, "My name is Ali."

Mandy looked at his face and replied, "That is a

very good name." She felt reluctant to tell him her name because it was the first time she had seen this man.

When Ali knew Mandy didn't want to tell him her name he said, "I just moved to the flat opposite your flat and I will be seeing you often."

"No problem," Mandy replied. Ali left Mandy and went back to his flat.

When Mandy entered her flat, she looked through her window to see whether Ali entered the flat opposite her flat or not. Unfortunately, Ali had entered his flat before Mandy looked through the window. She was a bit confused whether Ali was lying to her because the flat was quite empty for a long time. This didn't bother Mandy too much because that was the first time she had seen Ali.

After Mandy had made a cup of tea for herself, she decided to tidy her flat because there was stuff everywhere. As she was doing this and also enjoying her tea with cool music, someone rang her doorbell. Mandy was not expecting anybody and she thought it would be a salesman who wanted to sell a product. She ignored the bell and concentrated on what she was doing. The bell started ringing again and again, and then Mandy thought that Kate had changed her mind and decided to pay her a visit.

She went to open the door and see who was ringing her bell constantly. Surprise, surprise - Ali and his little boy were at the front door. Mandy was shocked and speechless, but before she could say anything at all the little boy asked, "Can we come in?" Mandy looked at his father's face and shook her head, "Yes, of course."

Mandy was not comfortable as Ali and his little boy, Ismaeli, entered. She showed them the living room to sit down. As Ali and Ismaeli sat down, Ali noticed that Mandy was not comfortable and he said, "I know that you just saw me today and you don't even want to talk to me. But I just feel I could talk to you because since I've moved to my flat, I can't see anybody to talk to. Everybody in this area keeps themselves to themselves."

Mandy intervened, "That is alright, what would you like to drink?"

Before Ali answered, Ismaeli said, "Soft drinks please," with a remote control in his hand, concentrating on changing the television channel. Mandy looked at Ali's face and smiled as Ismaeli hadn't allowed his father to answer. Mandy said, "Come on, follow me let us go to the kitchen and find a drink for you." She stretched her hand toward Ismaeli. Ismaeli stood up and held Mandy's left hand, and they both went into the kitchen while Ali was in the living room. Within two minutes Ismaeli came out of the kitchen with a can of seven up in his hand, while Mandy filled the tray with orange juice and cans of soft drinks.

Ali looked at Ismaeli and smiled, shaking his head left and right. Mandy noticed what Ali was doing and asked "Why are you shaking your head?"

"Every place he goes to it feels like home." Mandy smiled and placed the tray filled with orange juice and soft drinks on the table in front of Ali.

"Thank you very much," Ali said, smiling. Ismaeli sat down in front of the T.V with the remote control in his hand. He wasn't even listening to his father and Mandy's conversation.

After a few minutes Mandy said, "What do you want me to do for you, Ali?"

Ali looked at her face and replied, "I just want you to be my friend."

Mandy smiled and said, "If it's just friends that is okay with me."

Ali stretched his hand toward Mandy and she shook his hand. Then Ali said, "Friend!"

"Yes," Mandy replied.

Ali opened a can of coke and rose up with a funny voice and said, "A toast to our friendship!" Mandy looked at his smiling face.

Although Mandy had been surprised when Ali and his son turned up at the door, she continued talking to Ali. She felt relaxed. After an hour, Ali said to Ismaeli, "Let's go home; I need to relax a little bit."

Ismaeli replied, "Please Daddy, let's wait for some minutes because I'm enjoying my programme."

"You can go and watch it at home," his father said.

"It's boring at home," Ismaeli replied. He faced Mandy and said, "Please let me stay here to finish watching my programme."

Mandy looked at Ali's face and turned to Ismaeli. "Yes, of course you can stay."

Mandy stretched her hand towards Ismaeli and he held Mandy's hand. Ali stood up and walked towards the door. He looked back and said to Mandy, "Do you want me to leave him with you?"

"Yes, of course. You may come and collect him later."

"Thank you, Mandy. I'm very, very grateful. I will see you later." Ali opened the door and left. Mandy did not want to disturb Ismaeli because he was concentrating on watching his cartoon programme on T.V.

She said to him gently, "Do you want another drink?"

"No thanks. I haven't finished the one in my hand," he replied.

"If you need me I'm in the bedroom," she said.

"Okay," Ismaeli replied. Mandy left Ismaeli and went to the bedroom to relax. However, as Mandy lay in her bed, there was a question troubling her mind. Why did Ismaeli say their house was boring? Where was his mother? Had Ali he kidnapped him from his mother or did his mother abandon him? With all these questions in her mind, she fell asleep. After Ismaeli finished watching his cartoon programme, he also fell asleep on the floor in front of the T.V.

After an hour Mandy woke up and saw Ismaeli sleeping on the floor with a drink in his hand. Mandy laughed and carried him to her bed. Then Mandy picked up the telephone to ring Kate and to tell her about Ali. But when Kate saw that it was Mandy's number, she didn't pick up the phone. Mandy left a message on Kate's answering machine that she should call her immediately because she had good news for her. Kate was trying to avoid Mandy for what she had said to her. But she could not wait to hear the good news from Mandy's mouth. She rang her to hear about the good news. Mandy told Kate about Ali and his son.

"How did you come across this guy? Did he look handsome?" Kate asked.

"Yes, he is gorgeous," Mandy replied.

"What are you waiting for?" Kate asked.

"What do you mean by that?" she asked.

"Do you mean that he hasn't say anything to you at all?" Kate asked.

"No, he just left his son with me and said he will come back to collect him later."

"Where's his son now?" Kate asked.

"He is sleeping on my bed," she replied.

Kate laughed and said in a funny voice, "Automatically you've become his mother."

"That is funny," Mandy replied.

Kate said, "Seriously, would you like to befriend this guy?"

Mandy took a deep breath and replied, "I would not

mind if he dated me. But I need to take everything slowly and study him carefully."

Kate laughed and said, "What are you going to study in him, at least you fancy him."

"Yes, I know, but I do not want to fall into temptation again," Mandy replied.

As Mandy was talking to Kate, Ismaeli walked into the living room and Mandy said to him, "Do you want to say hello to my friend?"

"Yes!" he replied. Mandy said to Kate that Ismaeli wanted to say hello to her. Mandy handed the phone to Ismaeli to say hello to Kate. Ismaeli asked Kate what time she was coming to visit her friend so that he could see her. "Very soon," Kate replied.

"I will see you then," Ismaeli said and gave the phone back to Mandy.

"He is a very clever boy," Kate said to Mandy.

"He is!" Mandy replied." Kate promised Mandy that she would come around to see her new friend.

Immediately Kate put down the phone, her mobile phone rang and she picked the phone up to say hello. The man on the phone said to Kate that he was working for a courier company and he just wanted to confirm Kate's address because she had a parcel. Kate asked, "Where is the parcel from?"

"I think it's from New Zealand," he replied. Kate quickly gave the man her address and asked him the time he would deliver the parcel. "Tomorrow afternoon," he replied.

"I will be at home all day tomorrow. Please just ring the bell or give me a call when you're around."

Kate was pleased because she knew what was in the parcel. When Kate finished what she was doing, she went to Mandy's flat. As she rang the bell, Mandy opened the door. Then a voice came from the living room, "Is that my Dad?"

"No! It's my friend," Mandy replied. Immediately Ismaeli jumped up from where he was watching television to see Mandy's friend. "How are you?" Kate asked.

"I am fine," Ismaeli replied. "You are Kate?"

"Yes I am," Kate replied. They all entered the living room and as Kate was about to sit down, Ismaeli asked her, "What would you like to drink?" Kate looked at Mandy's face with surprise and Mandy used her shoulders to demonstrate that she should reply to him. "Orange juice," Kate replied. Ismaeli went to the kitchen and brought orange juice and a glass to Kate.

He put the drink on the table in front of Kate and said, "You can help yourself." He then sat down on the floor in front of the TV to concentrate on watching his programme. Kate looked at Mandy's face and said, "Thank you very much Ismaeli."

"You are welcome," Ismaeli replied.

After five minutes, Mandy excused Ismaeli, saying that she needed to talk to her friend in the bedroom; if he needed something, he should give her a shout. "That is alright," Ismaeli replied. Mandy and Kate went to the bedroom. Kate looked at Mandy's face and smiled as she wanted to say something. Mandy intervened. "Please do not say anything," Mandy said, smiling. Kate burst into laughter.

"I know what is on your mind," Mandy said. Kate looked at Mandy's face again and burst into laughter. Mandy could not control herself and she started to laugh as Kate continued laughing. They both laughed for about four minutes and Kate tried to control herself and said automatically, "You are his mother." Mandy looked at Kate's face as she was talking and burst into laughter again and Kate joined her; they both laughed for some minutes.

"Seriously, tell me your mind," Kate said.

"I have nothing in my mind," Mandy replied.

"What are you going to do with this guy and his father?" Kate said with a smile.

"I don't know," Mandy replied.

"His boy has taken you as a stepmother by looking at his reaction."

"Stepmother, no!" Mandy replied with a harsh voice. "I don't even know anything about them."

"Despite you not knowing anything about them, that doesn't warrant you not to be his stepmother," Kate said.

"That is very funny, Kate. What if his mother is around the corner watching her son, or if Ali still married to his mother?"

"That is what you need to find out," Kate said.

"Where am I going to find this out?" Mandy replied.

Kate smiled and said, "Talk to Ismaeli."

"What if he refuses to talk to me, or I upset him by asking him questions about his mother?"

"Then you will apologise," Kate said.

"If he refuses to accept the apology and tells his Dad, what do you think his Dad could do?" Mandy asked.

"He cannot do anything other than to stop talking to you or come to your flat," Kate replied.

Mandy took a deep breath and looked at Kate's eyes, and said, "I will try to ask him, but if it turns to disaster it's your fault." Kate smiled and they both went to the living room to meet Ismaeli. As Mandy and Kate walked to the living room, Mandy asked Ismaeli, "Do you want popcorn?"

Ismaeli pushed his nose up and took a deep breath. "That would be lovely," he said. Mandy looked at Kate's eyes and stretched her left hand toward Ismaeli and they both went to the kitchen to prepare popcorn for him. Kate stayed in the living room and lowered the volume of the television so that she could hear Mandy and Ismaeli's conversation.

In the kitchen, as Mandy poured some corn in the corn machine and it bubbled, Ismaeli jumped with joy and said, "The popcorn will be lovely." Mandy looked at his eyes and Ismaeli noticed the way Mandy looked at him and asked, "Why are you looking at me like that?"

With a low voice, Mandy bent down and replied, "Nothing, I just like how you are full of energy when you're jumping up."

"Are you going to allow me to come to your flat all the time?" asked Ismaeli.

"Yes of course, why not?" Mandy replied. She thought this was an opportunity for her to ask Ismaeli about his mother. She said to him, "What if you prepared to come to my flat and your mother stopped you from coming, what would you do?"

Ismaeli went silent for some seconds and Mandy looked at his eyes and said, "I'm very sorry for asking about your mother." Mandy tried to tickle Ismaeli to make him laugh. Ismaeli replied, "That's alright. I don't even know my mother. Mandy said to him, "I'm very sorry."

"That's okay," Ismaeli replied.

"Do you want to talk about it?" Ismaeli shook his head up and down. Then Mandy said, "After the popcorn?"

"Yes, yes," Ismaeli replied. By this time the popcorn was done, and Mandy poured it in a bowl and gave it to Ismaeli. Ismaeli smelt it and ran to the living room to meet Kate. "It is lovely," he said.

"Are you going to allow me to take some?" Kate asked.

"Yes, of course," Ismaeli replied. He brought the popcorn to Kate and Mandy stood by the living room door and watched him and saw that he was filled with joy. After Kate took some of the popcorn, Ismaeli ran to Mandy and said, "Have some, it is lovely." Mandy dipped her hands into the bowl and grabbed lots of popcorn. She wanted to see Ismaeli's reaction to what she had done. But Ismaeli said, "Take it." Mandy looked at his eyes and said, "I'm joking with you." She dropped the popcorn and Ismaeli looked at Mandy's eyes with a sideways look and smiled. "Thank you Mandy," he said. Ismaeli sat down in front of the T.V. and concentrated on watching his programme with one hand in the bowl of popcorn.

After some minutes, Mandy said to Ismaeli, "Do you need a drink?"

"Yes thank you Mandy," he replied. Mandy went to the kitchen to bring Ribena fruit juice to Ismaeli. Kate looked at Mandy's face, waiting for her to talk to Ismaeli about his mother. But Mandy felt reluctant because she didn't want to upset him and his enjoyment of the programme and the popcorn. Then Kate excused Mandy to the bedroom and said, "This is an opportunity for you to get something about his mother from him."

"Can't you see him happy with what he was doing? Do you think I'm going to make him miserable because of his mother's information? No, capital no!" Mandy said with a harsh voice.

"I'm very, very sorry, Kate said.

"I just want to help because I know that you like his father."

Mandy looked at Kate's eyes and smiled and gave her a cuddle. "I know that you are trying to help, but allow me to do this in my own time." They both smiled and went to the living room.

As Mandy and Kate entered the living room, Ismaeli looked at Mandy's face and asked, "Are you okay?"

"Yes, of course," Mandy replied. "Why do you ask me whether I'm okay?"

"Nothing," Ismaeli replied. Mandy looked at Kate's eyes and noticed that Ismaeli wanted to talk about something. She bent her hands deep into the bowl of popcorn, took some and placed it on Ismaeli's head. Mandy tickled Ismaeli to make him laugh. Ismaeli also put some popcorn on Mandy's head. They both tickled each other and started to laugh. Ismaeli and Mandy were playing around the living room, laughing and throwing popcorn at each other.

Ismaeli wanted Kate to join them, and he ran to Kate where she was seated and poured popcorn on her head. Kate joined them and they were all running around the living room playing with the popcorn. All the living room was in a mess with popcorn as they marched all over it. Ismaeli was so delighted and Mandy could see the happiness on his face. Suddenly, Ismaeli stopped and said, "Mandy wait, I want to tell you something." Mandy and Kate stopped to listen to him. In their mind, they thought he wanted to make a joke. But Ismaeli moved toward Mandy and placed his left hand on her shoulder.

"Do you know that you asked me about my mother in the kitchen earlier on?" Mandy looked at Kate's eyes and took a deep breath and answered, "Yes."

"I did not know my mother, but my father told me that he took me from her when she decided to forward her education. That is only what I know about her."

"Did your father make an attempt to take you back to see her where she was living?" Mandy asked.

"No, we did not discuss anything about her since my father told me that he took me from her because of her education."

Mandy cuddled him and said, "I'm very, very sorry."

"That is okay," Ismaeli replied. Then Kate threw popcorn to Ismaeli to cheer him up and make him forget about his mother. Ismaeli retaliated and they all started throwing popcorn to each other again.

As Mandy, Kate and Ismaeli were playing with the popcorn, the door bell rang. "I will get it," Ismaeli said.

"No, Ismaeli," Mandy replied.

"Why?" he asked.

"It might be a stranger," Mandy replied.

"Do you mean that I cannot open for a stranger?" Ismaeli asked.

"Yes, it may not be good for you to open the door for a stranger," Mandy replied with a low voice.

"Okay, okay," Ismaeli said. Mandy moved towards the main door and looked through the hole in the door to see who was ringing the bell.

She realised that Ali, Ismaeli's father, was the one who was ringing the bell. She opened the door for him. "What is happening here?" Ali asked when he saw the house in a mess. Mandy looked at Kate's face and Ismaeli's eyes and they all burst into laughter, then Ismaeli ran to Kate and scattered some popcorn on her head. Kate also pursued him with popcorn, then Mandy joined in and scattered popcorn everywhere. Ali was speechless and managed to sit on the sofa with popcorn on it.

But he could see that Ismaeli was happy. After a couple of minutes they stopped and Ismaeli turned to his Dad and asked, "How are you Dad? We are having fun."

"I'm fine thank you!" his Dad replied. "I can see that you are having a good time. Yes, of course that is great."

Then Mandy said, "Now it's time for us to clean up." Mandy went to the store cupboard and brought out the Hoover. Kate and Ismaeli were picking up the popcorn from the floor. Any time Ismaeli picked up the popcorn near where his Dad placed his legs he would say, "Excuse me Da-ddy." Mandy looked at Kate's eye and smiled. He said it more than three times and the way he said it was so funny. Mandy and Kate could not hold themselves; they looked at each other's faces and burst out laughing.

After they finished cleaning, Mandy offered Ali some drinks and immediately after Ali had finished the drink, he took Ismaeli and they both went to his flat. Mandy and Kate made fun of Ismaeli by repeating what he'd said to his Dad. Later Kate decided to go to her flat and Mandy escorted her to the car. "I will speak to you later," Mandy said.

"Take care of yourself," Kate replied and drove away. Mandy went back to her flat to have a little rest.

When Kate arrived home, there was a leaflet from the post man dropped into her letter box and it indicated that she had a parcel and she should phone them to arrange the time they could come to deliver it. Immediately Kate saw this, she rang the post office to find out whether she could come to collect the parcel. "Yes, of course," the lady who answered the phone said. Kate drove to the post office to collect the parcel. After collecting the parcel, on her way home she was full of joy. She knew the parcel was from Jackson and that it would be her ticket to France. Kate opened the parcel, her ticket and a postal order worth £10,000 pounds were there. Kate rang Mandy. Before she could speak to Mandy, she knew that something good had happened. "Mandy, I have got my ticket," Kate said.

"Who sent it to you?" Mandy asked.

"You know already who sent me a ticket," Kate replied with excitement.

"Was it Jackson?" Mandy asked.

"Yes, of course," Kate replied. "He didn't just send

tickets alone, he also sent a postal order worth £10,000."

"You're joking," Mandy said.

"No, I'm not. I will show you whenever I see you," she replied.

"You are a lucky bastard," Mandy said with a funny voice. "

Yes I am," Kate replied jokingly.

"Mandy, I will speak to you later because Jackson may be trying to get me on the phone." Kate ended the conversation with Mandy and jumped up and down several times for joy.

About an hour later, Jackson called Kate. "Did you receive your ticket?" he asked.

"Yes, darling, I received it. You are a genius. Not only the ticket, but a postal order worth £10,000. I don't know what to say. You are great Jackson," Kate said.

"That is alright," babe, Jackson replied. Before Jackson sent the tickets and the money to Kate, he had spoken to Robert, his friend, and told him, that his girlfriend was coming to France to enjoy the Cannes Film Festival and he should take care of her. Jackson told Kate the hotel she needed to stay in when she arrived in France, although Kate did not know that Jackson had paid for the hotel. She was thinking that the money Jackson sent to her would be used for booking the hotel. When they wanted to end their conversation, Jackson told Kate he would ring her in the airport before she boarded the plane. Kate thanked Jackson for the money and the ticket.

However, before Jackson sent the money, Kate had bought her ticket. What she did was to pay the money to her account. After Kate finished talking to Jackson, she called Mandy again and said, "Jackson has just hung up the phone now."

"Lucky you," Mandy replied. Although Mandy knew Kate's plan and what she was up to, she didn't want to upset her again by talking about her plan. Mandy believed that she would regret it later if everything came out.

A week later, Kate called Mandy and said, "I'm travelling tomorrow."

"Safe journey," Mandy replied.

"How are Ali and Ismaeli?"

"They're fine," she replied. Kate laughed. "Why are you laughing?" Mandy asked.

"I can see that you are in love with him," Kate replied.

"What do you mean by that? I haven't even sat down with him yet to talk about what he wants from me."

"You are killing yourself silently," Kate replied.

"Please, I don't want to discuss this matter further," Mandy said, and put the phone down.

Kate didn't bother whether Mandy put the phone down when she was still talking to her because she was filled with joy.

The day Kate was travelling, she woke early in the morning and packed her luggage,. although her flight took off in the afternoon at 2 o'clock, because she was so happy that she had fulfilled her plan to deal with celebrities for her revenge. Kate looked at the list of the names of celebrities she wanted to deal with and picked Robert's name. After she finished checking, she called a minicab to the airport. It was Friday and the minicab office was busy and they gave Kate twenty minutes to send a cab to her.

When the minicab arrived and the driver saw Kate in her dress, he liked her. "Madam, you look beautiful," he said.

"Thank you very much," Kate replied and walked

like a millionaire lady. "Could you help me to take my box to the cab please?" she asked.

"Yes, Madam," the cab man replied and ran inside to carry the box loaded with clothes and shoes. On the way to the airport, Kate's phone rang and she answered it. "Hello," she said.

"Where are you?" Jackson asked.

"I'm on the way to the airport, darling," she replied.

"The hotel car is waiting for you in the airport to take you to your hotel," Jackson said.

"You are joking," Kate replied with happiness.

"No, I'm not joking, I booked your hotel in advance before I sent your ticket," he said.

"Thank you very much, darling. What can I say, you are great."

"That is alright, I will talk to you in France," Jackson said.

"Thank you very much, bye," Kate replied.

The minicab man could see the joy on Kate's face when he dropped her at the airport. After Kate paid the fare, she asked the minicab man to keep the change. Kate was delighted with all her plans and how she was able to finance herself through Jackson. Immediately Kate landed at the airport in France, there was a limousine waiting for her to take her to her hotel. However, the driver didn't know who Kate was. But when Kate came out from departures and the limousine driver saw her, he could quickly recognise her. "Are you Kate?" the driver said.

"Yes, I am," she replied and pointed to her luggage. The driver quickly put the bag in the limousine and drove her to the hotel. Kate was given a celebrity welcome in the hotel by the hotel manager.

In the evening after Kate had relaxed herself, she called for the hotel manager. "Can I ask you some questions?" she said.

"Yes, of course," the manager replied.

"May I know how many celebrities book into this hotel for the Cannes Film Festival?"

"I'm very sorry Madam, that is a confidential matter," he replied in a polite manner.

"Thank you very much," Kate said.

"Is there anything I can do for you again, Madam?" he said.

"No thank you," Kate replied with a smile. The hotel manager left Kate's room.

Kate was a little bit upset that the hotel manager had kept information from her. She lay on her bed thinking what to do next. Then her phone rang – "How can I help you?" she said.

"You don't need to help me," Jackson replied with a funny voice. He was joking with Kate.

"Darling, I am very pleased and happy about what you have done for me," she said. "That's alright," Jackson replied. "Are you alright?"

"Yes, I'm fine, darling," she replied.

"I have given your room number to my friend Robert," Jackson said.

"Why did you have to do that darling?" Kate replied, pretending.

"Don't worry, he's my good friend. He will take care of you," he said.

"Are you sure of that?"

"Yes, I'm positively sure," Jackson replied,

"No problem if you are sure of that," Kate said.

"I will speak to you later," Jackson said.

"Bye, bye," Kate replied.

Kate was so happy that she had got the information she was looking for from Jackson, even though she'd pretended to ask Jackson questions, and inside her stomach she was delighted. She ordered some champagne and started to enjoy herself. Throughout that day, Robert did not visit Kate. Kate was drunk and fell asleep. She woke up in the middle of the night, sober and worried about whether Robert had come to knock the door. However, her surveillance equipment was not set up yet. She took the opportunity to set up her surveillance recording. She set two recorded cameras to face the bed and two in the bath room. Kate was confident that she was going to get Robert recorded in the bedroom and bathroom.

In the morning, Jackson rang Kate. "Have you seen Robert yet?" he asked.

"No, darling. Why are you so particular about Robert?" Kate asked, joking with Jackson.

"I have asked him to take care of you," Jackson replied.

"Do not worry, darling, I can take care of myself," Kate said.

"I know that you can take care of yourself, but there are lots of big guys there who could snatch you from my hand," Jackson said jokingly to Kate.

"Are you afraid of losing me?" Kate asked.

"Yes, of course," Jackson replied.

Please, darling, do not worry. I'm for you," Kate replied.

"Are you sure of this?" Jackson asked.

"Yes," Kate replied.

"Enjoy yourself and I will talk to you later." Jackson ended the conversation with Kate and Kate was delighted.

After Kate had finished talking to Jackson, she took her bath and dressed gorgeously. She walked around the hotel and later came back to her room. Anybody who saw her was quite sure that she looked beautiful. After a couple of minutes she went down to the restaurant to eat breakfast. Kate was enjoying her breakfast when the phone rang. She looked at the number and noticed it was a strange number. "Hello," she said.

"My friend, I have been into your room but you were absent," he said.

Kate couldn't identify who was speaking to her, but she knew that the voice was a man's voice. "Please, I don't want to be rude, may I know who is talking please?" she asked.

"It's me, Robert, Jackson's friend," he replied.

Kate pretended that she hadn't heard the name before. "Please sir, who is Robert?" she asked.

"Jackson and I work together in Hollywood," Robert replied.

"Please sir, may I know how you managed to get my number?" Kate asked.

"Please, I don't want you to be offended; Jackson gave me your telephone number, also your room number."

"Okay, I'm in the restaurant if you would like to come," Kate said.

"I'm sorry, my friend and I were on our way to visit a friend.

I will see you in the evening if you don't mind," Robert said.

"Yes, of course," Kate replied.

"See you later," Robert said.

"Bye," she replied. Kate had been careful not to ask Robert too many questions during the telephone conversation. Too many questions might put Robert off because he did not have it in his mind that he was going to do anything with Kate. He just wanted to know Kate as a friend, but Kate's mind was different.

Kate finished her breakfast with a smile in her face, and she went to her room and relax. She checked all her recording equipment because she was quite sure that Robert would turn up. The only problem she faced was how to make Robert, a married man, interested in her. To prepare for this Kate looked at her selection of clothes and also the best nice perfume that could attract Robert. After finishing dressing, she sat on the sofa chair waiting for Robert.

Unfortunately for Kate, Robert turned up in the evening with two friends. Immediately Robert knocked the door, Kate switched on the recording camera in her room because she thought Robert was alone, in order to record everything that they might discuss or anything that happened. But when she saw Robert with his friends she was disappointed. "Come in," she said.

When Robert and his friend saw Kate they were impressed with her looks. Kate ordered drinks and they all drank and they started discussing the films that would be the best of the year. They also talked about Jackson not being present at the Cannes Film Festival that year. Robert and his friends spent two hour with Kate before leaving to go to their rooms.

Robert promised Kate that he would come back again to check on her. "No problem," Kate replied. She was annoyed that her attempt to deal with Robert had failed the first time. But immediately Robert and his friends left the room, Jimmy, one of Robert's friends was interested in Kate.

"Robert, can I have her phone number, if you don't mind?" he asked.

"What! How can I give you her phone number, she is Jackson's girlfriend,"- Robert replied. Jimmy and his friend laughed. "What is so funny about that?" Robert asked.

"I just asked you for her phone number, there is nothing wrong with that," Jimmy replied.

Robert shook his head left and right and said, "Remember you are a married man." Jimmy started to laugh.

If I see your hands on her, I will tell Jackson and your wife," said Robert.

Jimmy laughed, -"My wife?"

Jimmy placed his right hand on Robert's left shoulder and tapped it three times and replied, "I know that you will not do anything stupid."

Kate was thinking about what to do next.

After Robert and his friends had left Kate's room, Robert rang Jackson to say he had seen Kate and she was doing fine. "Keep an eye on her," Jackson said to Robert.

The next day, Kate strolled out to see what the city looked like. She also visited the Cannes Festival Film Theatre where she saw lots of celebrities. In the theatre, Kate talked to many ladies and tried to make friends with them, but she was reluctant to give her phone number to any of them. On the way to her hotel, Jimmy saw Kate when he was inside his limousine and he asked the driver to stop.

Katie was also surprised when she saw the limousine stop for her. Then Jimmy came out of the limousine. When Kate saw him, she quickly recognized him.

"Jimmy where are you going?" she shouted.

"You know that we are in France because of the Cannes Film Festival. I'm going to the theatre," he replied.

"I've just come from the theatre now, I'm going back to the hotel because I'm tired," Kate said.

"No problem," Jimmy replied.

As Kate turned and was about to walk away, Jimmy said, "Kate." Kate looked back "I wouldn't mind paying you a visit, if it pleases you."

Kate took a deep breath for some seconds with chewing gum in her mouth, looked up and replied, "Em…em…it's ok."

"How can I get hold of you?" he asked.

"Take my number and give me a call, if you are coming," she replied.

"Thanks, Kate, I will give you a call." Jimmy entered the limousine and the driver drove him away.

Kate was happy to give Jimmy her number, because she thought if she couldn't get hold of Robert, Jimmy would pay the price. Jimmy was also delighted to get Kate's phone number, which Robert had refused to give him. Immediately Kate reached her hotel her phone rang,

"Hello, how can I help you?" she said

"Kate, how are you doing?" Mandy asked.

"I'm doing fine thank you." Before Mandy said another word, Kate intervened.

"You cannot believe the top Hollywood celebrities that visit me in my hotel."

"Lucky you," Mandy said.

"Which means that your plan is working"?

"What do you mean by that?" Kate asked. "Did you call me to insult me?"

"No," Mandy replied. "I just want to know how you are doing."

Kate replied in a funny way, "I'm fine, thank you."

"Now I have upset you. Why do you feel reluctant to answer me?" Mandy asked.

"I cannot say because you are my friend and I have told you all my plans, and my secrets, as a result you will be using it against me."

"I'm very sorry if I have upset you," Mandy said.

"That's alright," Kate replied.

"I miss you," Mandy said.

"I miss you too," Kate replied.

"Do you want me to pay for your flight to come to Paris?" Kate asked.

"But you're joking. No, no, definitely I will see you

in a week's time," she replied.

"Tell Ali that I said he should keep you company."

"Of course I will tell him," Mandy replied

"Thank you for your call and I will see you in a week's time," she said

"Bye, Bye" Mandy replied.

Fifteen minutes after Mandy called, Kate's phone rang again. By this time Kate was in the bath room having a shower. She ran to pick up the phone but the phone stopped. She took the phone with her to the bath room in case it rang again. Unfortunately the phone did not ring again before she had finished her shower. Kate looked at the phone to see the number, but the number was withheld. After she finished her shower she went to the restaurant downstairs to have some food, before she returned to her room. Kate had it in mind that she was not going anywhere for the rest of the day. As she lay on her bed watching some movies, someone knocked on her door. Kate was thinking that it was one of the hotel workers; and she moved to the door and asked,

"Who is that?"

"It's me, "Jimmy replied.

"I'm coming," Kate said. She went back to her bed without opening the door and put on some clothes because she only had on a night garment. Then she opened the door.

''You said that you were going to give me a call before coming," she said

"May I come in first?" Jimmy asked in a deep voice.

"Yes, of course," Kate replied

"I'm very sorry to disturb you but I did give you a call but you did not pick up the phone," he said.

"The phone stopped ringing before I picked it up," Kate replied.

"I'm very sorry," Jimmy said again.

"That's all right," Kate replied

"What can I offer you to drink?" Kate asked.

"Nothing at the moment," Jimmy replied

In Kate's mind she was delighted that Jimmy had showed up alone, although she was a little worried that Robert might turn up to see Jimmy there. This could jeopardize her chance of getting Jimmy again. Kate asked Jimmy several times what she could offer him to drink. But Jimmy just continued to decline her offers, because his aim was to get Kate in bed without letting Robert and the other friends know about it. Kate excused Jimmy to go to the bathroom, while she put on all her recording gadgets. In the bathroom, after she had put on her recording equipment, she took off her dress and came out with her night gown on. Jimmy could not resist.

"My God! You look beautiful," Jimmy said.

"Thank you very much," Kate replied with a polite voice. She walked towards the fridge in her room and brought out chilled champagne.

"Do you want this or a hot drink?" she asked.

"A hot drink would be better," Jimmy replied. Kate opened the drawer and brought out rum and poured it into two glasses. She walked towards Jimmy and gave him one glass and took the other. She raised her glass and said, "Cheers." With all the action, Jimmy pretended that he knew nothing. Then Kate sat down on the sofa opposite Jimmy, and crossed her legs with her drink in her hand.

"Have your drink," she said to Jimmy with a smile. Jimmy looked at her with narrowed eyes and smiled.

"Why are you smiling, Jimmy?" Kate asked

"Nothing," Jimmy replied. He looked at her again and smiled.

"Why are you smiling?" she asked a second time.

"I'm just admiring your beauty," Jimmy replied.

Kate looked at Jimmy with narrowed eyes, and smiled. Jimmy couldn't resist, he stood up and sat near Kate.

Without Jimmy knowing, Kate was recording every moment in the room. Kate looked at his face and said, "What do you want Jimmy?"

Jimmy looked at her and smiled.

"Say something, Jimmy," she said.

"I could not quantify how I admire you," Jimmy said.

"Do you know that you are a married man?" Kate replied.

"Yes I know, but something better is in front of me that I cannot reject," he said.

"What do you mean by that?" Kate asked.

"You are beautiful Kate; I'm really attracted to you."

Kate dipped her finger into her drink and gently put it on her tongue and moved it in and out in a sexy manner. Jimmy could not control himself, and he circled his left hand around Kate's neck and brought his lips closer to kiss her, but Kate declined his kiss and stood up. She held Jimmy's left hand and slowly moved towards the bed. By this time Jimmy could not imagine whether he was in paradise or not. He followed Kate, and she grabbed his head and gave him a dozen kisses. She slightly lowered herself onto the bed while Jimmy lay on top of her with a dozen kisses. They both rolled on the bed with a dozen kisses before they made love together. After they had made love Kate said, "I enjoyed that."

"It was great," Jimmy replied.

As they laid in bed Kate's mobile phone rang.

"Hello, how can I help you?" she said.

"It's me, Robert, if you don't mind I would like to come and pay you a visit, because I just received a call from Jackson."

"That's no problem," Kate replied.

"I'm on my way, I'll see you later,"

Kate quickly told Jimmy, as he got dressed and he said he would call her later. Kate kissed him and said goodbye. Jimmy quickly left to avoid being seen by Robert.

Kate quickly removed the cassette of her recording video and replaced it with a new one. She kisses the tape and said, "This will be lovely when I watch the action with Jimmy." After removing the tape, she entered the bathroom and had a good shower to prepare for Robert. After her shower Kate put on her best dress and moved around in the front of the mirror. She was so pleased with herself for the way she looked. She then sprayed the sweetest smelling perfume which had the smell of heaven on her body, that no man could ever resist . She then ordered a bottle of champagne in a freezing ice bowl. The hotel manager delivered the champagne by himself. Kate's phone rang.

"Hello, how can I help you?" she said.

"It's me, darling," Jackson replied on the other end

"Darling, thank you for everything," Kate said, pretending she was happy.

"You don't need to thank me," Jackson replied.

"I miss you very much," said Kate.

"I miss you too," he replied; "Have you seen Robert my friend?"

"He visited me once with some of his friends and promised me that he would come back to see me again.

But not so long ago, he rang me to say that he'd just received a call from you that he was coming to visit me".

"How did you enjoy the festival?" Jackson asked.

"It was great. I got the opportunity to know many celebrities I have read about in the magazines," Kate replied.

"You will know more than that when I marry you," Jackson said.

"Do you mean what you just said?" Kate asked with great joy, pretending she was happy.

"Yes, I mean every word I said," Jackson replied

"On that day, I will be queen of the universe," Kate said with a happy voice.

"I have to go now. I'll talk to you later," Jackson said.

"Thank you very much, my darling, for everything you have done for me; bye."

After the conversation, Kate's mind was in doubt whether Jackson really meant what he had said.

She was lying on the bed thinking about what Jackson had just said to her, when Robert knocked on the door. Kate regained herself and gently opened the door. When Robert saw her, he could not keep his mouth shut. "My God! You look so beautiful, Kate."

"Thank you very much," Kate replied with a huge smile on her face. "Come in." Robert walked in slowly and stood up. When Kate saw how slowly Robert walked in, she looked at his eyes with a smile on her face and said, "Sit down and feel comfortable."

"Thank you very much," Robert replied, sitting down on the sofa with a bottle of champagne in front of him.

Unlike Jimmy, Robert felt reluctant to get close to Kate because of his friend Jackson. Despite being attracted to Kate, he still saw her as his friend's girlfriend. Kate sat opposite Robert, crossing her legs, but sometimes she opened her legs on purpose to make Robert see her underwear. Despite all she was doing to win Robert's attention, he did not respond to the temptation.

"Robert the bottle of champagne is for you, if you don't mind," she said.

"Thank you very much," Robert replied.

"Do you want me to pour it in your glass?" she asked.

"No madam, I will pour it by myself," he replied

"That is very sweet of you to call me madam," she said.

"Remember that we are in France," he replied

Kate laughed. "Are you telling me that madam is in common language use for ladies in France?"

Robert looked at her and replied, "Yes madam."

Kate smiled and said, "You are an American; you need to use the American language and not French."

"I know that for sure, madam, but 'when you are in Rome you act as a Roman'" he replied.

"You are a very clever man," Kate said.

"Thank you very much," Robert replied with a smile. As Robert enjoyed the champagne with Kate they started talking about movies and life in Hollywood.

Deep down, Kate was not pleased with this discussion, but Robert was enjoying it simply because that was his business. Not only that, he also getting drunk and using the discussion to release the intoxication of the champagne in his body. Kate noticed that the way Robert was talking was not like before he had started to drink. She was determined to use this opportunity to lure him into bed. To start with, Kate ordered more champagne and this was delivered by the hotel assistant manager. Kate did not allow him to come in; she met him by the door. She also turned off her mobile phone in case Jackson called. Likewise, she persuaded Robert to switch off his mobile phone because they needed to enjoy themselves. Robert did not know what was in Kate's mind; he thought they were just enjoying each other's company. Maybe Robert would have known Kate's plan if she had not drunk with him. But Kate also drank heavily to confuse Robert; Kate did not usually drink alcohol but she was doing it in order to get Robert into bed.

After Kate saw that they were both drunk, she sat opposite Robert and opened her legs, pretending that she was not doing it deliberately.

When Robert saw her underwear he could not resist, he stood up and moved towards her. Kate looked at his face with love and stretched her left hand towards him. Robert gripped the hand and kissed it several times while looking at Kate's eyes. Kate replied with love. He kissed her and Kate also returned the kisses and they both gripped each other's clothes as they were moving towards the bed. By this time the tension was high and they both threw each other's clothes into different places. They had great sex that Robert really enjoyed; Kate also pretended to enjoy it too.

After sex, they lay on the bed talking about the sex and how great it was. Kate was happy to hear this because she was recording it, and Robert did not have a clue what was going on.

As they were in bed, Kate stood up to go and bring the champagne from the table. She poured it into two glasses, gave one to Robert and the other one for herself.

"Thank you very much, madam," Robert said.

"With your pleasure," Kate replied, with kisses. Kissing and romancing each other as they were drinking, they had sex again. During the sex, as Kate see that Robert was up to it, she used any system she could in the bed and Robert was happy with her performances. But Kate was doing this to get the best shots on the tape. However, Kate manipulated Robert to be talking during sex and he was shouting out like he was in heaven. All this action and talk Kate recorded on the tape.

Kate excused Robert to go to the toilet, and with delight Robert allowed her. Kate quickly entered the bathroom and set up the camera on the shower. When she came out she told Robert, "I need to shower, please, if you don't mind. Could you scrub my back for me?"

Robert was delighted and replied, "Your wish is my command". Kate gently opened the rope on her night gown, looking at Robert's eyes in the bed. Robert responded with a smile, waiting for what Kate was going to do. Kate gently removed his night gown and threw it on the sofa. She then stretched her left hand towards Robert and he replied with lots of kisses. They gripped each other with several kisses as they walk towards the shower.

Kate has already opened the shower, and water rained onto their heads. With several kisses, Robert could not hold himself back again, and they had great sex again. This time Kate and Robert were both shouting loudly as they were having sex.

After sex, Robert recommended the shower sex to be the best out of the three times they had had sex.. Kate was pleased that she had completed her assignment. They both showered together with lots of kisses.

Robert left and said to Kate, "I will talk to you later on the phone."

"No problem," Kate replied.

After Robert left, Kate jumped on her bed with joy because her journey to Cannes Film Festival had been a great success. However, Robert did not visit Kate again, simply because he later considered that having affair with her was a great mistake, but he still remembered how great Kate was in bed.

Jimmy called Kate again to arrange another visit but Kate declined because she had prepared the tape she was going to leave for Jimmy and Robert, and she thought any visit may jeopardise her chances. Robert talked to Kate on the phone several times, but Kate kept reminding Robert of the great sex they had had, although Robert did not want to talk about it.

When Kate finished recording the extra tapes that she wanted to give to Robert and Jimmy, she hid them under her bed. She strolled out for fresh air, hoping that nobody would see the tape. When the chambermaid came in to make the bed in the morning she saw the tape and called the manager.

The manager took the two tapes and put them in one envelope and took it to his office. When Kate returned she saw that the bed had been made. She quickly looked under the bed and the two tapes were not there. "Oh my God," she said and called the hotel manager. Immediately the manager received the call, he brought the tapes.

"Madam, is this what you are looking for?" he asked.

"Yes of course," Kate replied. "How did you manage to get hold of the tapes?" "The chambermaid called me when she found the tapes under your bed and I quickly put them in the envelope and took it to my office," the hotel manager replied. "Thank you very much," Kate said.

"With all pleasure," he replied and left the room. Kate viewed the tapes again and recorded some voices on it to make it sexy. She then put each tape in an envelope and addressed them to Jimmy and Robert.

She added a few lines of letter to each tape saying, " I really enjoyed the sex very much, which you will confirm by watching this tape, and I hope you also enjoyed it as well. This is to warn you that the master tape is with me, and I'm on my way home. If you do not want me to release this tape to the media, I want you to pay £100,000 into the account detailed at the back of this letter within one week. After you pay the money you need to call me, and give me the address to send the master tape to. Please, you need to give me at least a week after you pay the money into my account. Thanks, Kate."

Kate wrote the details of her account on the back of the letter and sealed the envelope. When she knew that the taxi was waiting for her downstairs, she called Robert and Jimmy and told them that she was leaving some envelopes with the hotel manager and that they needed to collect them urgently.

Kate handed the envelopes to the manager and said that Jimmy and Robert would come and collect them. She warned the manager that he should make sure that the envelopes reached their hands.

"Yes, madam, I will deliver it to them."

Kate entered the executive taxi to the airport and flew home with a smile on her face. When she was in the plane she recollected how her journey to Cannes Film Festival had been successful. She had fulfilled her dream to punish married celebrities to revenge her rape at the university.

Before Kate left France, she called Mandy to meet her at the airport. She told Mandy the time her flight would arrive at the airport. Mandy called Ali to escort her to the airport to pick Kate up.

"Could I come with Ismaeli?" Ali asked.

"Yes, of course," Mandy replied. "Who else are you going to leave him with?"

Ali laughed. "No one," he replied.

"I will be with you within five minutes," Ali said to Mandy on the phone.

"Okay, see you later," Mandy replied. She dressed up and went to the car to wait for Ali and Ismaeli. Ali and his boy were not aware that Mandy was in the car waiting for them. They were going to Mandy's flat.

Mandy tooted horn for them. Ali did not pay attention to the horn because he thought Mandy was in her flat. But Ismaeli looked towards where the sound was coming from and said to his dad, "Mandy is in the car waiting."

Ali looked and saw Mandy in the car. "How did you manage to see her?" Ali joked with Ismaeli.

Ismaeli looked at his dad with a sideways look and said, "Because I concentrate more than you, dad." Ali put his hands on his head to rough his hair and said, "That is my boy." Ismaeli looked at his dad's eyes and smiled. When Ali and Ismaeli entered the car and put on their seat belts, Mandy asked, "Are we ready?"

"Yes we are," Ismaeli replied. Ali looked at Mandy's eyes and smiled because she was playing reggae music and singing along with the CD on their way to the airport. After some minutes Ismaeli said, "Would you change the music please? Because it's boring."

"Young man, keep your mouth shut," Ali replied.

Mandy looked Ali's eyes and said, "Why did you ask him to keep his mouth shut?"

"There is no reason, madam," Ali replied.

Mandy smiled. "Do you know, I like him to speak out his mind."

"No comment, madam," Ali replied.

Mandy lowered the volume of the music and said to Ismaeli, "What music do you want?" "Destiny's Child or RnB," Ismaeli replied.

Mandy looked at Ali's face and asked, "Do you blame him?"

Ali shook his head left and right and said, "No."

"That is what he has grown-up with," Mandy said, raising her shoulders as body language.

"I cannot blame him because he was born in an advanced country- had it been he was born in a remote village where there was no electricity or any pipe water, he would not have demanded Destiny Child and RnB," Ali said.

Mandy laughed, "That is so funny," she said. "Please check the locker in front of you and pass me the latest Destiny's Child." Ali looked at the locker and gave Mandy the Destiny's Child CD, and immediately the CD started to play, Ismaeli was singing along with the music. Ali looked at how he was singing and shook his head and said, "Where did you learn how to sing this song, young man?"

"Remember that I watch Top of the Pops every Friday and also listen to the radio in my room," Ismaeli replied.

Mandy looked at Ali's eyes as he was asking Ismaeli questions and noticed how Ismaeli answered and she smiled. "Please allow him to enjoy the music," Mandy said to Ali.

"Thank you very much, Mandy," Ismaeli said. Ali smiled and shook his head.

After an hour's drive, Ismaeli said, "Mandy, I need to go to the toilet."

"Could you hold it for just three minutes until we arrive at the restaurant?" Mandy asked. "Yes of course I will wait," Ismaeli replied.

As Mandy drove to the restaurant car park, Ali said, "Maybe we could find something to eat before we leave."

Mandy looked at his face and smiled. "Were you hungry before?" she said.

"I did not eat anything before we left home," Ali replied.

"You could have told me before I took you to the airport with an empty stomach,"Mandy said.

"I am sorry, madam," Ali replied with a smile. Mandy parked the car and Ismaeli opened the car door and rushed to the toilet.

As Mandy and Ali went to enter the restaurant there was a cash machine, and Ali withdrew some money. They both went in and ordered some food.

"Do you want me to order some wine?" Ali asked.

"No, you know that I'm driving," Mandy replied. She looked at his face and smiled. "Thank you very much, I really appreciate your offer."

As Mandy and Ali were waiting for the waitress to bring their food, Ismaeli came out from the toilet. "What do you want to eat, Ismaeli?" Mandy asked.

"I love chicken burgers," Ismaeli replied.

"Come, let's go and order you some food." Mandy took Ismaeli by the hand to the desk where she ordered food for him. After they had finished eating they bought some soft drinks and biscuits for the car. They drove to the airport, while Ismaeli enjoyed the music played by Mandy.

Kate's flight arrived on time. Mandy, Ali and Ismaeli were waiting for her in the airport. When Kate saw Ali and Ismaeli with Mandy, all the excitement in her mind that she wanted to tell Mandy about, in the car on their way home disappeared. However, Kate was not disappointed to see Mandy and Ali come to the airport together to pick her up because she knew that the feeling between them was strong. Immediately Ismaeli saw Kate in the distance, he ran to meet her.

"How was your journey?" he asked.

"Very good," Kate replied.

"Did you buy anything for me?" he asked.

Kate looked at his eyes. "Yes, of course," she replied. She stopped and opened the side of her suitcase zip and brought out some packets of chocolate. "Take it, it's for you," she said. Ismaeli took the chocolate and ran back to Mandy and Ali who were moving towards Kate.

"She bought a packet of chocolate for me," he said, raising the chocolate.

"Lovely," Mandy replied. Ali looked at Ismaeli as he was shouting because of the chocolate and shook his head, smiling. By this time Kate had joined them.

"Welcome home, my friend," Mandy said with a funny voice, and cuddled Kate. "How was your journey?"

"Great," Kate replied. As Mandy wanted to ask another question, Kate said, "Allow me to say hello to Ali." She moved towards Ali and cuddled him "Thank you very much for following her to pick me up at the airport."

"With all my pleasure," he replied.

Kate looked at Mandy's eyes and smiled.

"What are you smiling at?" Mandy asked.

"You cannot deny that he is taking good care of you," Kate replied.

They all burst into laughter.

Mandy looked at Ali's eyes and said, "Are you sure that the statement is true?" Ali smiled, and before he could say a word, Kate intervened: "I am not an idiot you know!"

Mandy laughed and replied, "I know that. Come let us go home."

Ali took Kate's suitcase from her hand. "Thank you very much," Kate said.

As they were walking towards the car, Kate looked at Mandy's eyes with the side of her eyes and looked at Ali and smiled. She did this several times. Mandy noticed what Kate was doing and kept smiling until they reached the car. Mandy pressed the key to open the car. Kate wanted to sit in the back seat; Ali insisted and said, "You and your friend have many things to chat about."

Ali opened the back door and sat with Ismaeli, while

Kate sat in the front with Mandy. "How was your journey?" Mandy asked.

"It was great, everything went according to the plan," Kate replied. Mandy looked at Kate's face and shook her head left and right while smiling. Kate noticed what Mandy was doing and said, "What do you mean by that?"

"Nothing," Mandy replied.

Kate ended the conversation so that Ali would not be aware of what was going on.

"Did Jackson call you?" Mandy asked.

"Yes, of course," Kate replied.

"He is a great man," Mandy said. Kate looked at Mandy's eyes and shook her head up and down. "I know," she replied.

Mandy was not aware of what Kate had in store for her. She said in a low voice, "I think you did not do anything stupid this time."

Kate looked at her face and looked back to see whether Ali might be aware of what they were saying, and she replied, "I have two great tapes to show you when you come and see me."

Mandy looked back and saw what Ali and Ismaeli are doing. By this time Ali was sleeping. Mandy shook her head and said, "Until you fulfil your fantasy."

"Yes, of course, I have already told you that someone will pay for what those stupid guys did to me. Now I don't want us to talk about this anymore, just come and see me anytime. You have less to do."

Mandy was thinking in her mind that if Kate did not stop what she was doing, it might affect her relationship with Ali if he knew what was going on. Also, Mandy did not want to lose her best friend. Kate already had it in mind that the journey to Cannes Film Festival was the end of her revenge with married celebrities. She was thinking of getting serious with

Jackson.

As Mandy was trying to park in front of Kate's flat, Kate's mobile phone rang. When she looked at the call the screen showed a private number, and she decided not to answer the call. After Mandy parked, Kate's phone rang again and showed a private number. Then she decided to move a little away from the car and answer the call. "Hello," she said. Jackson replied on the other end "I have called before and it went into voicemail."

"Sorry, dear, my friend just parked the car and we just came out from the car. I heard the phone ringing, but it stopped before I could answer it."

"Are you alright?" Jackson asked.

"Yes, I'm fine, darling," she replied.

"I just called to find out whether you arrived home safely," Jackson said.

"Thank you very much, darling, for caring about me," Kate replied.

"You know that I've always cared about you," he said.

Kate laughed and replied, "Yes, I know."

"Did you enjoy your trip to Cannes Film Festival?" Jackson asked.

"It was lovely, dear, your friend Robert and his friends made me feel at home. Please help me to thank them," Kate said.

"I will do that for you," Jackson replied. "Let me leave you, darling, to go and have a shower and relax yourself."

"Thank you very much dear, I will talk to you again," Kate said.

"Bye, bye," Jackson replied.

Kate moved toward Mandy, Ali and Ismaeli and said, "I'm very sorry to keep you waiting. The call was from Jackson."

"No problem," Ali replied, but Mandy looked at Kate's eyes and smiled. Kate saw the way Mandy looked at her and smiled, and she said to Mandy, "Do not start again." Ali and Mandy helped Kate to take her bag to her flat.

Inside Kate's flat, Kate said, "You know that I've just arrived from travelling and I have no food at home, but I could order you pizza, if you do not mind." Before Kate finished, Ismaeli intervened and said, "That would be great." Kate ordered a pizza and some drinks..

Meanwhile in France, the hotel manager delivered the two tapes to Robert and Jimmy separately. Immediately Robert read the letter in the envelope with the tape, he was shocked. He quickly went to his room to watch the tape. When he saw what was inside the tape, he was very annoyed and continued to swear bad words.

Robert did not want to rush anything at all; he kept the tape in his suitcase and tore up the letter. He lay on his bed thinking about what to do next. As Robert was thinking about the next step, he fell asleep. Then his phone rang, "Hello," he said.

"Robert, I couldn't believe what this bastard girl has done to me," Jimmy said.

"Who are you talking about?" Robert asked, pretending that he was not aware what was going on.

"This bastard Kate," Jimmy replied.

"What has she done to you?"

"She recorded everything I have done with her on tape," Jimmy replied.

"What do you mean by everything, Jimmy?" Robert asked.

"You know, you know.", Jimmy couldn't spell it out that he had had an affair with Kate.

But Robert knew what had happened. "Did you

have sex with her?" Robert asked Jimmy. Jimmy kept silent for about two minutes before he said "Yes."

"But I told you that she was Jackson's girl friend," Robert said.

"I have made a bloody mistake," Jimmy replied.

"What are you going to do now?" Robert asked.

"I don't know! She demanded £100,000 to be paid into her account within two weeks, otherwise she will send the master copy to the national media."

"Give her a call and ask her what she wants," Robert said.

"I am going to do that right now," Jimmy replied, and ended the conversation.

Robert realised that Kate was using the sort of blackmail to make money and she could do worse if her demand was not met.

Jimmy gave Kate a call on her mobile Kate looked at her mobile and saw Jimmy's number. "How can I help you?" She asked.

"You bastard, I will kill you if I get hold of you," Jimmy said with annoyance. Kate laughed and replied, "Did you think you could use me? All this rubbish you are saying on the phone, if you fail to pay the money into my account within two weeks, your name will hit the headlines in the newspapers. And I'm very sure that all the Hollywood gossip magazines would love to hear about the story and see the tape." Jimmy was furious with the way Kate spoke to him on the phone, immediately he realised that Kate was pleased with what she had done to him, and also she meant business if he did not pay this money into her account.

Jimmy called Robert and told him about the conversation with Kate.

"Did she agree to send the master tape to you?" Robert asked.

Jimmy took a deep breath and replied, "She means

business."

"What do you mean by that?" Robert asked.

"She was so serious about what she was doing, that she planned it well before she started to execute the plan," Jimmy replied.

"What are you going to do now?" Robert asked.

"She wants me to pay some money into her account," he replied.

"How much did she ask you to pay into her account?" Robert asked.

"A couple of grand," Jimmy replied.

"How much?" Robert continued to ask.

"One hundred thousand pounds," Jimmy replied.

"That is not too much," Robert said, pretending that he was not aware of what was going on.

"How are you going to get the master tape back from her?" Robert asked.

"She swears to God that if the money is paid, she will send it by courier to me," he replied.

"Do you believe her?" Robert asked.

"The way she was talking, I believe her."

"Where are you going to receive the tape?" Robert asked.

"I'm going to make the payment now so that I can receive the master tape before I leave France," Jimmy replied.

Robert laughed and said, "You don't want to go to America to receive the tape because of your family."

"This is a disaster, my friend," Jimmy replied, with a low voice.

"I warned you that Kate was Jackson's girlfriend, and you should not have anything to do with her," Robert said.

" I should have listened to your advice," Jimmy replied. "Friend, I will see you later, let me go and make this payment."

Meanwhile, Robert did not tell Jimmy about his own ordeal with Kate and Jimmy was not aware of this also. Immediately Robert finished the conversation with Jimmy, he went to the bank to make the transaction. After he'd finished with the bank, he called Kate on her mobile phone. He told Kate to go and confirm the next day. Kate swore to him that she would send the master copy by courier tomorrow, immediately after she'd confirmed that the money was there.

"Thank you very much," Robert said.

"You are welcome," Kate replied.

The following day after Kate finished all that she was doing at home, she went to the bank to confirm the payment.

When she saw that Robert and Jimmy had paid the money into her account, she was delighted and made individual calls to get the address where she would send the master tape to. They both gave her the address they would be available to collect the tape on arrival. Robert kept this secret from Jimmy, he knew about Jimmy's ordeal with Kate. Truly, Kate sent the master copies to Robert and Jimmy, which they received in France before travelling to Hollywood after the Cannes Film Festival. Although they received the master copy from Kate, still they did not trust her. They left France after destroying the tapes by hand. In their mind they put their finger across that Kate would not do anything stupid.

Mandy did not have time to spend with Kate yet to find out what she had come with from France, and whether her plans had been successful or not, but she felt Kate was in a good mood when she picked her up from the airport. Also, Mandy and Ali were in a good relationship, which gave Mandy less time to spend with her friend Kate. Now Kate had fulfilled all her plans, she brought out the pictures of celebrities she had cut from magazines to punish because of her rape, and she destroyed everything. Although Kate could have continued her plans further to punish more celebrities, she was stopped by the pressure from Mandy, her friend, and Jackson, who she considered to be a great opportunity in her life, that might not come again. She thought twice and stopped her plans to concentrate on her relationship with Jackson.

Kate had got money in the bank and she left her job to plan the next stage with Jackson. This was going to be good news for her friend Mandy and also for Jackson, who was looking forward to knowing more about Kate. But how Kate was going to cope with the celebrity status , was another thing entirely. However, Ali had proposed to Mandy to marry her and Mandy had accepted. Mandy and Ali planned a weekend visit to Kate to tell her that they were going to marry each other. When Kate called Mandy during the week, Mandy told her that she had got good news for her., but she was not going to tell her until the weekend when she saw her.

"I cannot wait to hear the good news," Kate replied.

Although it was in Kate's mind to tell Mandy that she was going to be serious about her relationship with Jackson, she cautioned herself not to tell her during that conversation. She preferred to tell Mandy when she visited over the weekend. Also, during the week Jackson talked to Kate about how she could come and visit him in New Zealand before he finished filming. But Kate declined and said she preferred to visit him in America when he'd finished filming. Jackson was happy about Kate's proposal and promised her that she would not regret it when she visited.

Before the weekend, Kate brought out the tape she'd recorded when she was having sex with Jackson in

New Zealand. She watched the tape and destroyed it. After destroying the tape, she burnt the film to make sure there was no trace of it.

At the weekend Mandy, Ali, and Ismaeli visited Kate to tell her about their plans to get married. It was a great weekend because Kate had prepared for their visit. Mandy and Ali told Kate how they loved each other and they needed to make their feelings official. Kate was so happy for Mandy and wished them well. But deep down, Kate was wondering how Mandy was going to cope with Ali's religion. She could not say this to Mandy in the presence of Ali, so as not to upset her. As they were enjoying themselves with wine and fried chicken and meat, while Ismaeli concentrated on the box of chocolates that was on the table, Ali said, "I know that is not going to be easy for Mandy to convert to Islam, but if love is there every other thing will follow."

Kate was pleased to hear this statement from Ali. She turned to her friend Mandy and asked, "What do you think about Ali's statement?"

"I have thought about it several times, I know that it's not going to be easy, but this is a sacrifice I want to make and there is no turning back."

Ali looked at Mandy's face as she was talking, held her hand and kissed her several times, cuddled her and said, "I love you." Kate was moved and saw that they were in love.

After some minutes Kate said, "Mandy I have good news for you." Mandy left what she was doing and paid attention to Kate so as to hear the good news. Kate laughed when she saw how Mandy paid attention.

Mandy said, "Please, please, Kate, I cannot wait to hear the news."

Ali looked at Kate and Mandy, how they were cracking jokes and smiling. Then Kate said, "I have decided to be serious with Jackson."

Mandy could not wait for Kate to finish, she jumped and shouted for joy and cuddled Kate with the words, "That is great, that is great." Then Mandy opened a non-alcoholic wine and poured it in her glass, Kate's glass and Ali's glass. She then raised glass up and said a toast to "my best friend Kate for her great news."

As Mandy went to pour the drink into her mouth, Kate intervened and said, "Also a toast to my best friends Mandy and Ali for their great news." Kate and Mandy looked at each other's faces and laughed. Ali was pleased for them and smiled whenever they both cracked jokes. Mandy, Ali and Ismaeli enjoyed their weekend with Kate and left for Mandy's flat. On the way home, Ali said to Mandy, "I could see that your friend was very happy this weekend, when I first knew her, she wasn't like that."

"She is a lucky girl," replied Mandy. "But what I am worried about is how she is going to cope with the media when they find out that she is Jackson's girlfriend."

"She is mature enough to cope with that," Ali replied.

"I really pray for her that everything will go well between her and Jackson," said Mandy. "Don't worry about her." Ali held Mandy's hand and looked at her face.

Mandy smiled and said, "I will stop worrying about her."

"Good!" Ali replied.

Two months later, Robert decided to give Kate a call to thank her for not sending the tape to the media. Kate's phone rang. "Hello, how can I help you?" she said.

"How are you doing?" Robert said.

"I'm fine, thank you," Kate replied. She did not

recognise Robert's voice, and she said, "May I know who I'm speaking to please?"

"It's me, Robert."

"How are you doing, Robert?" Kate asked.

"I am fine, thank you," he replied.

"Did you receive the tape I sent to you?" Kate asked.

"Yes, of course," Robert replied.

Before Robert said anything, Kate intervened, "Robert, I want to apologise for what I have done to you. I'm really sorry about everything."

Robert was surprised to hear this from Kate. "Are you serious about what you are saying?" he asked.

"I swear to God with all my heart I am serious," Kate replied. "That's why I sent the master tape to you. Please forgive me."

"I have forgiven you, please do not involve yourself with this type of rubbish again," Robert said.

"Yes, I will not anymore, thank you," Kate replied.

When Robert ended the conversation with Kate he was delighted that the case had ended. Robert wanted to call Jimmy and tell him what Kate had said to him, and how she apologised for what she had done to him.

But he realised that he hadn't told Jimmy that he'd slept with Kate. He then decided to give Jimmy a call to ask him about his matter with Kate. Jimmy said to Robert that the matter had died and he didn't want to think about it anymore. But Robert replied, "How can you be sure that the matter has died? What about tomorrow, if she demands more money from your hands, what are you going to do?"

"What do you want me to do now?" Jimmy asked.

"Give her a call and pretend that you want to thank her for not giving the tape to the media," Robert replied.

"That is a very good idea, I will give her a call and

get back to you," said Jimmy. He was not sure how Kate was going to react if he called her, but he hoped for the best.

After Jimmy was less busy, he called Kate. "Hello, how can I help you?" she said.

"How are you doing?" Jimmy asked.

"I'm fine, thank you," she replied. "Please may I know who I am speaking to please?"

"Jimmy," he replied.

"Oh my God, Jimmy, how are you doing?" Kate asked.

"I'm fine, thank you," he replied.

"How is your family?"

"They are okay," he replied.

"Please Jimmy, I just want to say I'm very, very sorry for what I did to you in France."

"That's alright," Jimmy replied with shock.

"So, have you forgiven me?" Kate asked.

"Yes, of course," Jimmy replied.

"Are we friends again?" Kate asked.

"Yes, of course," Jimmy replied with surprise.

"I will see you when I come to visit Jackson," said Kate.

"See you then. Bye, bye." Jimmy was over the moon that this matter was not going further anymore.

With surprise, he gave Robert a call and told him how Kate apologised to him.

"Now you can put your mind to rest that the matter is gone," said Robert.

"Do you know that she is coming to visit Jackson?" Jimmy said.

"She may be the lucky one as Jackson is free to do anything he likes," replied Robert.

"Do you mean because he is divorced?" Jimmy asked.

"Yes, of course," Robert replied.

"But he could have waited for all this gossip about his divorce to die down before making a move," said Jimmy.

"As far as I'm concerned, he is a free man," Robert replied.

Kate and Jackson discussed Kate's visit to Hollywood in depth in order to avoid embarrassment and they talked about how to tackle the media and Hollywood gossip. Kate understood what she wanted to go through and started preparing herself for the outcome of the visit. Mandy visited Kate and they both discussed what would happen when the news came out. Mandy was so pleased that Kate understood what she would go through, if her visit were known to the media. The most joyful moment for Mandy was when Kate showed her how she'd destroyed her pictures of celebrities, collected for the revenge of her rape. From that moment, Mandy believed that Kate has changed for good. Although, Mandy was planning her own wedding with Ali, they were both happy for each other.

"In about a few month's time, we shall say men are not bastards, but today we are happy to be with them," Kate said.

Mandy laughed and replied with a funny voice, "My mother always said, 'Do not say never because your "no" today maybe your "yes" tomorrow.' They both laughed. As they were about to start another gossip, Mandy's mobile rang, and she looked at the screen and saw that it was Ali's number.

"Hello dear, what can I do for you?" she said.

"I need your attention now, if you do not mind," Ali replied.

"I'm on my way. I will see you later," she said. "Kate I will see you later."

"Say hello to Ali and Ismaeli for me," Kate said to Mandy.

"Bye bye. I will give you a call when I reach home," Mandy said.

"No problem," Kate replied.

Kate and Jackson talked to each other by telephone all the time to plan Kate's visit. Her visit was kept secret between Kate and Jackson. Also, those who knew about the visit like Jimmy, Robert and Mandy did not discuss it with anybody.

As the days went by, Kate and Mandy were counting the days to when Kate was going to visit Hollywood. Meanwhile, Jackson had told Robert that he was having a big visitor.

"Who is that visitor?" Robert asked, pretending that he didn't know what was going on.

"It's my girlfriend, Kate, from London," Jackson replied.

"Do you mean the one I saw in Cannes Film Festival in France?"

"Yes," Jackson replied.

"Do you mean that it's going to be the lucky one?" Robert asked.

"I think so, who knows tomorrow?" Jackson replied.

My friend, I know that you know what you're doing and what could make you happy."

"Thank you very much Robert, I will inform you when she arrives," Jackson said.

Immediately Jackson had finished talking to Robert, his mobile rang. It was Jimmy.

"Who were you talking to?" Jimmy asked.

"I have just finished talking to Jackson," he replied.

"I have been trying your mobile, but it was engaged. I wonder who you were talking to," Jimmy said.

"I just told you now that I was talking to Jackson," Robert replied.

"What were you talking about?" he asked.

"He told me that he's having a visitor."

"Do you mean Kate?" Jimmy asked.

"Yes, of course," Robert replied.

"We are going to see how this relationship is going to end in disaster," Jimmy said.

"What do you mean by that?" Robert asked. "Are you praying for Jackson not to settle in his life again? Or are you telling me that after his bitter divorce he should not marry again?"

"No, I'm not saying he should not marry again, but he's not someone Kate should settle down with," Jimmy replied.

"Are you telling me because you have slept with her, she is a prostitute?" Robert said.

"No, I'm not saying that."

"What are you trying to say, tell me," Robert said.

"Em.. em.. em..! You know that she did to me wasn't fair," Jimmy said.

"Please, I do not want to continue with this conversation because Jackson deserves to be happy," Robert said.

"Ok, I will talk to you later," Jimmy replied.

"Bye," Robert said.

However, Robert was avoiding discussing Kate's matter because it reminded him of what Kate had done to him. So far, Kate had apologised and was serious with Jackson in their relationship, and he wanted them to be happy when she visited Jackson in Hollywood.

Jackson played down Kate's visit so that it would not leak to the press. But this was short lived when Jackson hired a limousine to pick Kate up from the airport. Although Jackson did not go to the airport with a limousine, the media were packed at the airport to see who Jackson's visitor was. Jackson had discussed with Kate that he was not going to come to the airport with the limousine. But he described the limousine colour and what the security was to wear. Also, Jackson described what Kate was going to wear to the security. However, Kate's flight was delayed by thirty minutes. The driver waited for her because the probability that the flight could be delayed was paid for by Jackson, so the driver had no problem with waiting. When Kate's flight arrived at the airport, the security and the driver acted quickly to protect her from the media. When Kate saw the amount of media that were flashing their cameras to take her picture, she was shocked. Although she'd prepared for the media she was not aware that there could be as many as she saw in the airport. Also, Jackson's house in Hollywood was surrounded by the media. When Kate arrived in , the limousine entered the compound where media was not allowed by the security.

But to the media's surprise, after thirty minutes Jackson and Kate came out to speak to them. Jackson had warned Kate not to say anything, that he would do the talking. As they were speaking to the press, some of the journalists tried to question Kate, but she replied with a smile. Jackson and Kate spent fifteen minutes speaking to the press, before they went inside.

The following morning, newspapers carried Jackson and Kate's picture all over the world. Kate was not comfortable with all this publicity, but there was nothing she could do about it, although she'd thought she was prepared for the coverage by talking to Jackson about the publicity of the media. After seeing the amount of publicity in the papers, magazine, news and internet every day, she was not comfortable with the coverage. But Jackson stood by her and give her emotional and moral support. After a week, the publicity start to die down, as Jackson had predicted to Kate before she'd arrived in Hollywood. Kate thought this was the time to give her best friend Mandy a call to tell her how she was coping with the situation in

Hollywood.

Mandy told Kate that she would be alright. She also assured Kate that all the publicity in London was dying down. Mandy advised Kate to keep it cool with Jackson and she should not think about rushing home because of the media. However,, the first and second weeks Kate visited Hollywood were not enjoyable because of media coverage. Also, she was not going out with Jackson so as to avoid media snappers.

After two weeks, Jackson and Kate started visiting some friends, and also went shopping together with a security guard. However, the media were not leaving them alone, but it was better than the first and second weeks. Kate enjoyed her visit to Hollywood, and she also kept in touch with Mandy to tell her everything that was going on in Hollywood.

One evening, after Kate had spent four weeks in Hollywood, Mandy returned from work tired; she lay on her sofa and her mobile rang. It was Kate. She was happy to receive the call. "Are you okay?"

"Yes, of course," Kate replied.

"How is Jackson and all his friends in Hollywood?" They're all fine."

"How did you deal with the media coverage?"

"It was terrible," she replied.

"But my man helps me through all the terrible moments."

"We saw you how you remained silent throughout the media interview."

"You are joking," Kate said, with an embarrassed voice. "Do you mean that the interview was broadcast in London?"

"Yes, of course," Mandy replied.

Kate take deep breaths in and out.

"Do you know you are visiting one of the most powerful men in Hollywood?" Mandy asked.

"What do you think my parents will say about me?" Kate asked.

"Do you want my opinion?" Mandy said.

"Yes, of course," Kate replied.

"If I were your parents…" Before Mandy could start to talk, Kate intervened: "You are not," with a joking voice.

Mandy laughed and replied, "I'm not your parent but I am your best friend."

"Yes, I know, continue your statement, best friend," Kate said jokingly.

"If I were your parents, I would be over the moon," Mandy said.

"Please do not kid yourself," Kate replied.

"I am very serious."

"Please tell me the reason why you need to be over the moon when your daughter is being broadcast in the news around the world?"

"But you are not being broadcast for murder or anything bad, you are only being broadcast for visiting one of the most powerful men in Hollywood," Mandy replied.

"Do you think my parents could be proud of that?" Mandy laughed. "What is so funny about this?" Kate asked.

"There is nothing funny about this," Mandy replied. "In my opinion, I will say yes, because they do not know what may happen tomorrow, whether you may be his wife."

Kate took a deep breath and said, "I do not know what I would do without you."

"Do you remember the time we said all men were bastards?"

"Yes, of course," Katie replied.

"The tables have turned, it's now time for us to enjoy," Mandy said. "You're a great and fabulous friend to me. I want you to enjoy yourself to your fullest in Hollywood, and remember to buy a present for me when you are coming back home."

"I will do," Kate replied.

As Kate went to say goodbye, Mandy said, "I forgot to tell you something, it just came to my memory."

"What is that again?" Kate asked with a funny voice.

Mandy laughed and said, "Remember that when you come back to London you are going to face media publicity again."

Kate laughed and replied, "I know, let me deal with Hollywood first before thinking about home."

"That is brilliant," Mandy said. "Enjoy yourself and I will tell Ali and Ismaeli that I've spoken to you."

"Goodbye, I will talk to you another time," Kate said.

Kate was a little relieved after she'd talked to her friend Mandy about what she was going through in Hollywood. After this, she considered giving her parents a call, but she was not sure whether it was appropriate to do so. After discussing this with Jackson, she was advised to wait until she got back to London, when the media were not watching her anymore. Kate enjoyed her quality time with Jackson, and also Jackson did not regret having Kate as a guest in Hollywood. Jackson took Kate to many places, include VIP parties, to let all his friends know he was with her. He even planned in his mind to propose to Kate, but he later realized that the first visit might not be appropriate because Kate might consider it to be too quick. He wanted Kate to enjoy her first visit to Hollywood, and to discuss the second visit with her later. Jackson's mind was to marry Kate if she accepted.

He did everything he could do to impress Kate, for her to accept his invitation to visit him a second time in

Hollywood. Kate was pleased with the way Jackson treated her as special for the couple of weeks she spent with him. She even prayed to God in her mind for Jackson to propose to her and she would say yes. Kate was also on her best behaviour to impress Jackson. Jackson praised Kate for the way she handled the media publicity and also the way she behaved to his friends in Hollywood. Although both of them wanted the same thing, they expressed it to each other through love; they were both nervous to say it to each other verbally.

One day, Kate and Jackson were alone in the dining room, eating, and Kate looked at Jackson's eyes with love and gave him a kiss. Jackson replied with dozens of kisses. Kate was carried away with the kisses and started taking off Jackson's clothes and throwing them anywhere as they were moving towards the bedroom. Jackson could not remove his tongue from Kate's mouth until they got to bed and made love. After a few minutes they finished making love and Kate said, "Let us go back to dining table to eat our dinner."

They both went back to the dining room and started laughing about the way both of them couldn't insist on each other finishing their dinner before making love.

After some time, again Kate looked at Jackson's face with love and said, ''Thank you very much for the special treatment you give to me. I don't know what I do to deserve this special treatment.''

"It is alright, I just try my best for the lady I love."

Kate looked at his eyes and smiled, and said, "Thank you."

Kate bent her head to her right shoulder and looked at Jackson's eyes and said with a loving voice, "Would you accept my second invitation?"

With a smile on his face, Jackson stood up and saluted, and replied with a deep voice, "Yes, madam."

Kate jumped up and circled her hands round

Jackson's neck with dozens of kisses. Both of them could not control themselves, and they dragged themselves to the bedroom to make love again.

Kate spent five weeks with Jackson in Hollywood. Jackson used the last week to do shopping for her. The last day before Kate wanted to leave Hollywood, Robert and Jimmy paid a surprise visit to her. Robert just wanted to say goodbye, but Jimmy had another thing to say to her .

Before Robert and Jimmy arrived at Jackson's home, they had given him a call. He was so pleased because his friends were coming to say bye to his fiancée. Immediately Robert and Jimmy entered Jackson's home, they saw Kate lying on Jackson's lap on the sofa in the living room.

"I can see happiness on your face, friend," Robert said.

Jackson smiled and said, "Kate is going tomorrow."

"We've just come to say goodbye to her," Robert replied.

Kate lifted her body up from Jackson legs and said, "Thank you very much." As Jackson, Robert and Jimmy chatted in the living room, Kate was not comfortable with their chatting. She excused herself and went to the kitchen.

After two minutes, Jimmy excused himself to go to the toilet. Jimmy's intention was to talk to Kate in private about his money. On his way back from the toilet he saw Kate in the kitchen, and he moved towards her and said, "I hope you are coming back a second time to visit our friend." He said this for Jackson and Robert to hear from the living room.

Robert said, "Definitely, she is coming back."

Jackson smiled, without knowing what was going on in the kitchen.

Jimmy whispered into Kate's ear and said, "I will be

waiting for my money if you do not want me to expose what you have done to Jackson." Jimmy quickly moved out of the kitchen to join Robert and Jackson in the living room, so that Jackson would not suspect what was going on. Immediately Kate heard the statement from Jimmy, her eyes changed dramatically. Her mind was troubled because she was getting used to Jackson and she didn't want to lose him. She walked to the living room and pretended that nothing had happened. Jackson quickly identified that something was wrong with Kate.

"Are you alright, darling?" he asked.

"Yes, I'm fine, thank you for caring." She moved towards Jackson and sat on his lap, looked at his face with love and gave him kisses.

When Robert and Jimmy saw the love and passion between Kate and Jackson as they were kissing each other, Jimmy said, "You are going to miss her very much." Jackson, with a smile on his face, replied, "Yes, of course."

Kate looked at Robert and Jimmy's faces with a smile and said, "I am going to miss you guys." She paused and looked at Jackson's eyes with love and said, "I will come back to visit you again very soon."

On the following day, Kate left Hollywood to return to London with fear in her mind whether Jimmy was going to reveal her secret to Jackson. When Kate was on the flight she was still worried about the situation until she landed at London Airport. Immediately Kate's flight landed at Heathrow International Airport, lots of media were waiting for her. She tried what she could to avoid the media but they kept following her. Kate covered her head with a scarf to avoid her picture being taken by the photographers and the media until she was able to get to a mini-cab.

Kate could have asked her friend Mandy to come

and pick her on her arrival into Heathrow International Airport, but she feared exposing her to the media. Before Kate left Hollywood she spoke to Mandy about her decision not to allow her to come and pick her up on her arrival, and they both agreed in order that she and Ali would not be exposed to the media. However, in the conversation between Mandy and Kate, Mandy made it clear that she wanted Ali to go to Heathrow to pick Kate up, and Ali had agreed to do so. Kate refused blankly because she did not want to put Ali and Mandy's relationship under media scrutiny.

Throughout the week Kate returned from Hollywood, she was on the tabloid front pages. She could not step out because of paparazzi surrounding her flat to get hold of her picture. She ordered her food and what she needed through the internet and they delivered the stuff to her at home. Kate also talked to Mandy and Ali about staying away because of paparazzi. When Kate arrived from Hollywood, she become a big celebrity in London. She talked to Jackson all the time to give news about her flat been surrounded by paparazzi. Jackson gave her moral support on the phone how to deal with the publicity and tabloids. Jackson also apologized to Kate for letting her go through all this hassle. Any time Jackson apologized to Kate about the media publicity, she was not comfortable with it because she was determined to go through this with Jackson. Also, Jackson promised to give her the best love and be a good man to her.

It took Kate two months to live a normal life after returning from Hollywood. She couldn't go out shopping without being afraid of the media or paparazzi. She quit her job to avoid gossip at work, also to avoid her story being sold to the tabloids by her work mates.

Kate gave her parents a call after she came back

from Hollywood for more advice and they were a great help to her. She promised to visit them in the countryside, but they advised her not to come because of the local media. Kate visited Jackson in a secret location in America where he was filming his latest movies after the media publicity had died down.

Jackson's friends could see the relationship between Kate and Jackson was serious, and they all supported him. Jackson did not only deal with Kate's media pressure ; he was also dealing with his former wife selling her story to the media and magazines in order to discredit him. Jackson found it tough to be reading the story about his former wife in the magazines at the time he knew Kate. But he was determined to stick to his new relationship with Kate, whatever may be the case.

Jackson had separated from his former wife before he met Kate. He also filed for divorce against his wife. He knew that the divorce would cost him lots of money but he was determined to get rid of her from his life for good. Jackson wanted to settle his divorce with his wife out of court, but his wife insisted on going to court. Not because of money, but because of publicity to tarnish Jackson's reputation in t Hollywood. It took two years for Jackson to finalize the divorce settlement with his wife because of the daughter involved. Jackson's divorce put Kate in the streamline of media publicity and magazine coverage, but Kate stood by Jackson till the divorce from his wife was finalized.

After the divorce papers came out, Jackson and Kate got engaged secretly, but this was later leaked to the press after two weeks. Immediately the media published their engagement, Jackson announced that he was getting married to Kate. This was not a new story to the media anymore, because they saw how Kate had stood by Jackson throughout the divorce procedure.

The only news the media were expecting from Jackson was to give the day and the date of the marriage. Kate had been visiting Hollywood frequently to support Jackson when the divorce procedure was in court. But after Jackson settled the divorce from his former wife, she decided to move to Hollywood to join him. Despite the treatment of his former wife, Jackson was pleased with Kate's courage, physical and moral support during the divorce procedure.

Robert and Jimmy saw Kate all the time in Hollywood, but Jimmy did not give up trying to collect the money he gave to Kate to silence her when he had an affair with her in France during the Cannes festival. Robert did not want to hear about the affair anymore because he had made up with Kate and also promised her that they would forget about it totally. Robert also advised Kate not to bother about Jimmy's treatment of her; however, Kate couldn't get it out of her mind. The first time it was known to Kate that Jimmy had told Robert that he had had an affair with her, she was worried whether Jimmy had told another friend. But Robert assured her that Jimmy would not risk his marriage by telling anybody. However, Robert warned Jimmy not to jeopardize the relationship between Kate and Jackson because of $100,000. Jimmy gave Robert the option of paying the money if he wanted to be a good man, or a Good Samaritan to Kate. But Robert refused on the basis that Jimmy had slept with Kate for the price of his money. Meanwhile, when Kate saw that Jimmy's treatment was getting to her, she told Robert that she would tell Jackson about her affair with Jimmy.

Robert told Kate to wait, and that he would speak to Jimmy about the treatment. When Robert saw_Jimmy, he said to him: "Jimmy, do you know that Kate is going to tell Jackson that she slept with you?"

"That is fantastic," Jimmy replied with a funny laugh.

"What are you laughing about?" Robert asked. "Are you going to jeopardize your marriage because of a silly affair?" Jimmy continuing laughing.

"I need my money," said Jimmy. But inside himself, he was worried about ruining his eleven year marriage because of a silly affair with Kate.

Robert moved towards Jimmy with one hand in his pocket and another hand pointing to Jimmy's face. He lost his patience and started to exclaim and said, "I have tried enough for you, but you did not pity yourself." Robert shook his head left and right with funny body language and said, "Now the ball is in your court whether to save your marriage or ruin it with a silly affair."

"What do you want me to do now?" Jimmy replied angrily. Robert tapped Jimmy's shoulder and whispered in his ear and said, "Use your common sense to resolve what is between you and Kate before it escalates". As Robert turned away from Jimmy, Jimmy said, "I will not ask her the money anymore."

Robert looked his face and replied with a smile, "Good for you."

"How do you think I can make up with her?" Jimmy raised his voice as Robert had moved away from him.

"Go and apologize to her, as you have placed her in a terrible situation," Robert replied.

However, it took Robert lots of courage to persuade Kate not to tell Jackson about her affair with Jimmy. Also, it took him the same courage to change Jimmy's mind about blackmailing Kate with money. After Robert left, Jimmy quickly looked for one way or another to go and apologize to Kate. Robert, Jimmy and Kate became close friends in Hollywood and promised each other not to talk about the affair anymore.

Despite enjoying Hollywood, Kate did not forget her friend Mandy, although they were thousands of miles away from each other. She called Mandy all the time and talked about what was going on in Hollywood. Also, Mandy gave Kate all the information about what was going on in London.

The media and the Jackson fans were waiting for the date Jackson was going to choose for his wedding. Jackson and Kate discussed the wedding day, and it took them three months to come out to the media. While all these arrangements were going on, Jackson flew Kate's parents to Hollywood for them to agree to the date and the time. Although Jackson talked to Kate's parents all the time by phone, sometimes they met at a secret location arranged by Kate in order to avoid the media.

The day Jackson announced the wedding day, it was circulated throughout the whole world. The only disappointment to the media was that the wedding would be covered by the magazine which had signed a contract with Jackson and Kate through Jackson's agent. However, lots of media tried to negotiate a deal with Jackson's agent but the deal was signed with only one magazine company. There was lots of security put in place by the magazine company, so that no media would secretly enter the venue on the day of the wedding.

From the day Jackson and Kate announced their wedding to the wedding day was about three months and four days. This gave the magazine company lots of time to prepare for the policing of the wedding.

After the announcement, Jackson's agents were bombarded with proposals to organise the wedding. When the agent reported to Jackson, he selected one of the agents who had been dealing with the Hollywood wedding. Jackson and Kate's wedding announcement was in the media for only a few weeks because it was not new coverage to the media. Jackson and Kate had to deal with their look on the wedding day. They both agreed that they wanted to look simple on that day. Jackson hired one of the Hollywood female top designers to deal with Kate's look and also hired one of the Hollywood male top designers to deal with his own look. Although the wedding was still months ahead, Jackson and Kate did not take anything for granted.

Throughout the midst of the wedding preparation, Kate discovered that she was pregnant. When she first discovered she was pregnant, she did not want to tell Jackson, simply because she did not want to put him under media pressure again. Also, she thought the news could affect Jackson during his filming for his latest movies; but Kate called Mandy, her best friend, to tell her about the pregnancy. Mandy shouted for joy and she was over the moon when Kate told her.

"How did Jackson feel when you told him?" Mandy asked.

Kate took a deep breath. "I am not telling him yet," she replied.

Mandy was silent for some seconds and asked, "What are your reasons for not telling him?"

"I don't want to put him into the media spotlight again," Kate replied. "Also, I don't want to disturb his attention because he is filming his latest movies."

"But you still need to tell him or do you want him to hear from another person?"

"No, no, that will be unbearable to him," Kate replied with a harsh voice.

"Then you need to tell him," Mandy said.

"Okay, I will tell him tonight," Kate agreed.

"Please tell me, how are you going to tell him?" Mandy joked with Kate. "Are you going to tell him in a romantic voice or a sleepy voice?"

"In a romantic and sexy voice," Kate replied. Mandy laughed. "Has that answered your questions?" Kate said with a sexy voice.

"Yes, of course" Mandy replied.

"Mandy, I have to go now. Say hello to Ali and Ismaeli for me".

"Bye Bye," Mandy replied.

After Kate put down the phone, she was thinking about how she was going to tell Jackson, and whether Jackson would say it was too early for her to have a baby or be happy with the news. Kate was troubled in her mind as she was meditating how to tell Jackson about the pregnancy, when Jackson entered. He moved towards Kate where she sat on the sofa and kissed her three times. "Are you okay?" he asked.

"I'm alright," Kate replied. Before Jackson said anything, Kate said, "Honey come and sit down with me. I need to discuss something with you".

Jackson looked into her eyes with love and jumped onto the sofa. "I cannot wait to hear what you want to tell me," he said.

"Do you think you are not going to be upset when I tell you what I want to tell you?" Kate asked.

Jackson used his right finger to touch Kate's nose with smiling love and replied, "What could make me annoyed with my dear?"

"Nothing, nothing". Jackson attempted to carry Kate up from the sofa. Kate tickled him and they both ended up on the floor.

Jackson looked at Kate's eyes with love and gave her more kisses. Kate responded by circling her left hand around Jackson's neck and using her right hand to hold Jackson's right hand and gently drawing it to rub her stomach several times. Jackson stopped and looked at her eyes with surprise and asked, "Do not tell me that you are pregnant?" Kate looked at his eyes and paused for some seconds and replied, "Yes, yes". Jackson jumped up and started running round the house with the joyful words, "I'm going to be a father again." Kate lay on the floor looking at him with a smile and happiness. After a couple of minutes, Jackson returned to Kate and kissed her several times, lifted her up with both hands and ran around the house with the words, "We are going to be parents." Kate was delighted because of Jackson's reaction to her news of pregnancy.

After Jackson settled down, Kate asked, "Jackson can I ask a question?"

"Yes, of course" Jackson replied with a smile.

"Do you think my pregnancy is going to affect your filming for your new movies?" Jackson looked at her eyes and touched her nose. "What do you mean by that question – mother to be?" he asked with a smile on his face.

Kate looked at his face, inhaled, and said, "What I mean by that question is that could you concentrate on your filming while thinking of me and your baby?"

Jackson laughed. "Yes of course, I will always be thinking of your and our baby".

As Kate was about to ask another question, Jackson intervened. "Do not ask me whether this is going to affect my concentration when filming." Kate looked at him with love and laughed. "You have read my mind," she said.

"Honey, I have been in this business for a long time and also this is a double blessing from God. My filming is going well and we are expecting a new baby."

Kate stood up from the floor and sat on the sofa and said, "I'm hungry, starving."

Jackson looked at her face with a smile and asked, "What are you going to eat, mother to be?

I will prepare the dinner."

Kate, full of love and smiles, smacked him with the

181

back of her right hand, and said, "It's too early, let me perform my duty. Do not spoil me."

Jackson replied, "Honey, I'm not spoiling you because of this – I just want to give my baby special treatment."

"Okay sir – I will be with you in the kitchen," Kate said with a smile and love. Jackson prepared a good dinner for Kate and himself. After dinner, Jackson discussed the wedding preparations with Kate and how to pay for the contractors and the contractors' progress. Jackson and Kate did not want to tell anybody about the pregnancy because they did not want media attention. The only problem for Kate was the wedding gown. She needed to tell the designer that Jackson hired for her. Jackson knew that Kate's pregnancy could leak from the designer's team – he asked Kate's designer to sign a confidential agreement through his agent.

Kate's parents called her all the time to find out how she was getting on with her wedding. The following day, after Kate had told Jackson about her pregnancy, her parents called.

"Kate, how are you and Jackson doing?" Kate's mother asked.

"We are doing well," Kate replied. How is my dad doing?"

"He is with me as I'm talking to you."

"Could I speak to him please?" Kate asked. Kate's mother gave the phone to her Dad.

"Dad are you okay?" Kate asked.

"Yes, of course we are okay."

"Dad, I need to tell you something."

"Okay!"

"I'm pregnant," Kate said. Kate's Dad was silent for some seconds. "Dad, are you there?" "Yes, my daughter," her Dad replied. Kate's Dad started to cry for joy.

"What is the problem?" Kate's Mum asked her husband. She grabbed the phone from her husband. "Kate, what did you say to your Dad that made him cry?" Kate kept silent. "Talk to me, talk to me," Kate's Mum repeatedly said to Kate.

Before Kate opened her mouth, her Dad said, "She is pregnant."

"Oh my God! Is it true Kate?"

"Yes Mum," she replied.

"Thank you God," Kate's Mum said. "How many months?"

"Mum, I cannot tell."

"Have you told Jackson?"

"Of course, Mum. Is he happy about it?"

"He was jubilant," Kate replied.

"I cannot wait to see you in your wedding gown with a big stomach," Kate's Mum said and laughed jokingly.

"Please my daughter; be careful with anything you are doing."

"Did you hear what your Dad said?"

"Mum," Kate replied.

"He said you should be very careful with whatever you are doing now."

"Yes, Dad," Kate replied.

"Mum, I have to go now – I will speak to you and Dad another time."

"Bye bye," Kate's Mum said.

Kate put down the phone with a big smile on her face. As she put down the phone, Jackson opened the door, and saw Kate with a big smile on her face. He asked: "Have you won the lottery? I can see a big smile on your face."

"Yes, of course," Kate replied. Before Jackson spoke, Kate intervened with a smile, "If it's a money

183

lottery we don't need it because we have enough, but if it's a baby lottery, yes I am going to be a Mum." As Kate went to continue talking, Jackson stopped her with several kisses. Kate looked at his face with love and smiled and said, "I love you."

Kate and Jackson kept a low profile about the pregnancy because of the media publicity. Although Kate told her friends and her parents about her pregnancy, she knew they would keep it to themselves.

As Kate and Jackson's wedding day got closer, Kate's stomach was getting bigger. All the agents working for her wedding were brilliant. Jackson called Kate all the time from the site where he was filming his latest movie to assure her that everything would be fine. Even with all the assurances Jackson gave to Kate, she still worried about her wedding day.

Kate's worries were due to two reasons – her affair with Robert and Jimmy, and how Jackson would react to the news if it came out. The second worry was about Jackson's ex-wife, if she managed to get in on the day of the wedding. Although Jimmy and Robert had promised Kate that everyone should forget the past and move on, could they change their mind because of the money involved and put their marriage into the media spotlight? A few weeks later, Jackson finished his filming and came back home.

Kate was delighted to see Jackson come back home because she had been at home alone throughout the period of Jackson filming his new movies. She did all her shopping on the internet and everything was delivered to her. After Jackson finished his latest movie and returned back home, their wedding day was less than four weeks away. After exhausting himself during his movies, it should have been time for Jackson to rest. But he needed to be on the phone always to see how everything about the wedding was going on. Jackson had two things to worry about - whether the wedding was going to be successful; also, whether Kate was going to cope with the pressure of that day with her pregnancy. Most of the time, if Jackson was on the phone, Kate would come to him. He would be at her back, using his right hand to hold the phone on his ear and the left hand to rub her stomach. Kate was delighted with this type of romance, although sometimes in her mind she questioned herself, did she deserve all this good treatment she was receiving from Jackson?

Sometimes Jackson would ask her what she was thinking – she would reply, "Nothing, I am just overwhelmed."

Kate and Jackson were delighted with the agents that handled their wedding arrangement. Everything was in place two weeks before the wedding day. Also, the arrangement for Kate's parents – the hotel where they were going to stay in order to avoid media attention and the car to pick them up from the airport when they arrived, everything was in place. Kate also made arrangements for the hotel and the car to pick up her best friend Mandy and her partner, with Mandy's stepson Ismaeli.

Kate did not find her pregnancy easy because it was her first child. She was sick and vomiting all the time. The best news was that she got the best private doctor visiting her at home all the time. A week before the wedding day, Kate was sick and vomiting seriously. Jackson was so afraid – he was thinking of postponing the wedding, but Kate said no. Kate's doctor was called during the middle of the night. After treatment, she was looking better the following day. Jackson asked Kate whether she could cope with the wedding pressure. Kate gave him the assurance that everything would be okay. The agent organising the wedding received many calls from the media to reveal the details of the wedding to them with an offer of a sum of money. But they refused the offer because they had signed a confidential agreement with Jackson.

The Reverend that was going to marry them, and all the guests, had been informed that the wedding would take place at the same venue as the reception. Jackson and Kate would tie the knot and the reception part would start.

Kate had no experience of weddings and how stressful they could be, but to Jackson this was his second wedding, and he knew about the pressure of a wedding until everything is finished. That was the reason he asked Kate all the time if she could cope with the pressure along with the pregnancy, and Kate found the question irritating sometimes. Jackson, being someone who had gone through that pressure before, would take time to explain to her. When Kate was sick and a doctor was called in, Jackson asked Kate whether she wanted them to postpone the wedding: "Because what I care about is you and our baby in your stomach." But to Kate, the wedding was so important to her. However, the baby was also important to Kate, but the wedding was what Kate hadn't dreamt of because of her ordeal in university, and for her to have an opportunity to marry was something that was very important to her. This was the reason why Kate was doing everything she could do to prove to Jackson that she could face the pressure.

On the wedding day, Jackson and Kate had agreed with the agent in charge of their wedding that they were going to use a hotel to get dressed before going to the wedding venue. Jackson and Kate had visited the hotel secretly to avoid media attention. Also, the Reverend who would be marrying them had visited them in their home. The agents that organised the wedding are on top of very thing. This made Jackson and Kate delighted about everything.

The day before the wedding day, at the dinner table, Kate looked at Jackson's eyes with love and smiled. With a deep voice, Jackson asked, "May I know what the mother of my baby is smiling about?"

Kate used the fork in her hand to demonstrate a microphone and said with a funny voice and body language, "Will you, Kate, take Jackson as your perfect husband?" Jackson stopped eating and concentrated, looking at her face with a big smile on his face. "Yes, I do," she said. She changed her voice and said the opposite. "Will you, Jackson, take Kate..."

"No, no," Jackson intervened, "That is not the way you are supposed to say it." Then Jackson took his fork to demonstrate a microphone and said, "Will you, Jackson, take Kate, the perfect mother of your baby, to be your wife; love her for better or worse. Yes, I do."

They both laughed and Jackson looked at Kate's face with love across the dinner table and gave her kisses with the words, "I love you very much."

Meanwhile, Robert, Jimmy and Jackson's friends were planning what to do on the day of Jackson's wedding to make it special. This was because they knew what he had gone through during his divorce from his former wife. To see him happy again – they wanted to do something funny on the day; they planned to buy whistles to blow on the day. They were planning to stand up when the Reverend asked the question, "Is there anybody in the audience who opposes Jackson and Kate being joined together – to speak now or hold their silence." Three of them would stand and look at each other – just to get the attention of Jackson. They knew he would concentrate on them – to hear what they were going to say. Jackson knew Robert, Jimmy and Vivian couldn't disorganise his wedding day because they were good friends.

Not only that, they were the people standing by Jackson when he was going through a terrible divorce from his former wife. Also, for Jackson to wed Kate – Jackson had sought their advice – they both know what was going on at the wedding. Vivian was the one who had recommended the agent that organised Jackson and Kate's wedding.

A day before the wedding when Robert and Jimmy visited Jackson in the hotel, Jackson saw whistles in their hands.

Immediately he knew that they were planning something for his wedding. When Jackson asked them, "What are you doing with the whistle?" Robert replied with a funny voice that it was for a friend. Jackson smiled and said jokingly, "If you embrace me in front of my guests, I will kill you." Robert and Jimmy looked at each other and laughed and laughed. They made funny jokes with Jackson – tomorrow would be a special day for all of them. Jackson was delighted with Robert and Jimmy for coming and cheering him up a day before the wedding in his hotel. Vivian also wanted to visit Kate in her hotel to cheer her up, but Kate did not know their plan. There was a song Robert, Jimmy and Jackson sang in anything they filmed together. When Robert and Jimmy visited Jackson in the hotel, as they were about to leave Robert started the song:

"Do not listen what people talk about you.

Do not listen what people talk about you.

They may talk good about you.

They may talk bad about you (x2).

Please do not listen what people talk about you."

Immediately Jimmy and Jackson joined him, and they both started singing the song as usual. After they had finished singing the song, Robert and Jimmy said goodbye to Jackson. "We will see you tomorrow on the big day." Jackson was deeply moved by Robert and Jimmy's action in the hotel. He didn't want them to go, but they had to leave him to have enough rest for his big day.

A day before the wedding, at night in the hotel, Jackson dreamt about his former wife, and that she had breached security and come to the wedding reception with a baton and started smashing all the drinks and the wedding cake. As the security was trying to stop her, she smacked them with the baton. In the dream, Jackson saw that everybody was running away from her until one security guard wrestled her down. When Jackson woke up on the wedding day his mind was troubled. In the morning he called Robert and Jimmy to come and see him immediately in the hotel. When Robert and Jimmy arrived he told them about the dream. They laughed at Jackson, when he asked them what was funny about the dream. Robert replied, "Friend, because you are nervous about this wedding, simply because you don't want anything to go wrong."

"You may be right," Jackson said, "but prevention is better than cure."

"We will do everything to support the security to make sure she cannot come in," Robert and Jimmy assured Jackson.

"Thank you very much, friends," Jackson replied. Robert and Jimmy left the hotel to go and prepare themselves for the wedding.

On the wedding day, the agents organising Kate & Jackson's wedding agreed with them that they both needed to be at the wedding venue thirty minutes before the starting time. The wedding would start at 1:00 pm and Jackson and Kate had to be there at 12:30 pm. The limousine that carried Kate arrived exactly on time, but Jackson could not arrive on time because there was a shooting accident on his way and the traffic

189

had to be diverted to another route. The route Jackson's limousine was diverted to there were lots of traffic which caused the lateness of Jackson. All through this, the agents working with Jackson were able to communicate with the ones working with Kate about their situation and Kate was informed. As Kate's limousine was waiting in the front of the wedding venue and many guests are waiting inside to see the bride and groom, many things were going on in Kate's mind.

When it was exactly 1:00 pm and Jackson had not arrived, Kate thought he had run away. As she was thinking this, the Reverend who was going to marry them came out from the venue to look around to see whether Jackson and Kate had arrived. He saw Kate's limousine but he could not see Jackson's car. He sent security to go and ask Kate what was going on. This added worry to Kate's mind. She was sweating in the limousine – the agents working with her gave her cool water to drink because they could see that she was not herself. As they were attending to her one worker looked at the window and saw Jackson's limousine. Kate looked through and saw him arrive. She said jokingly, "I will kill him if he runs away." They both laughed. Jackson stepped out on the red carpet walked in with his best man to take his seat in the front of guests.

The lady who coordinated the wedding came out to Kate's limousine and said, "It's now time for you to come in – everybody is waiting to see you." Kate replied with a happy, funny voice, "Yes M'am!" Meanwhile, Kate's father was waiting for her to enter by the door, to hold her hand in order to give her to Jackson. As Kate stepped through the door her father looked at her – how gorgeous Kate was in the wedding dress – tears of joy dropped from his eyes. Kate stretched her hands towards her father and her father held onto her hands. Looked at her face, he shook his head up and down and said, "This is my daughter, you look beautiful." He kissed her forehead and said again, "You look beautiful." Kate's father put Kate's right hand on his arm and they both started walking into the venue.

As Kate, with her father and flower girl at the front and best lady with the rest of the girls, stepped into the hall, everybody stood up and the piano men playing melodious songs for them. As they walked towards the altar Kate's father handed Kate to Jackson in front of the Reverend and took his seat. Immediately, Kate was handed to Jackson, the piano stopped. The Reverend said everybody may be seated. Meanwhile, Robert, Jimmy and Vivian had taken their seats at the front closer to where Jackson and Kate stood. The hall was quiet as the Reverend conducted the marriage service. Then he asked the audience the question whether anybody opposing the joining of Kate and Jackson together should speak now or hold their peace forever. Robert, Jimmy and Vivian looked at each other's faces and stood. As the three of them were standing there was a noise in the hall. Everybody concentrated on them and what they were going to say. Kate quickly demanded a chair, so as not to collapse. Her best lady quickly gave her a chair to sit down.

Kate's father stood up, sweating, with worry on his face. Jackson composed himself because he knew Robert, Jimmy and Vivian, who were the brains behind the wedding, could not destroy their handiwork. The Reverend stopped looking at them – with a sad voice he said, "Brothers and sisters, what are your reasons not to let Kate and Jackson be joined together?"

Robert faced the audience and said, "We do not have any reasons for Jackson and Kate not to be joined together; we just want to show our loyalty and support to them." Then he turned to Jackson and looked at his face emotionally and they both said, "Friend, you chose the best lady in the world." After he finished the speech, they started blowing the whistles. The audience could not stop laughing. Jackson could not control his emotion – he told the Reverend, ""Excuse me," and he came to Robert, Jimmy and Vivian and cuddled them. "Thank you my friends," Jackson said several times. By this time, Kate also couldn't stop laughing. Kate looked at Vivian's eyes with a smile and shook her head. Vivian signalled to her with his eyes and finger and said, "I got you!"

"I will kill you when I've finished this wedding," Kate replied jokingly.

After some minutes, Jimmy raised his voice, walked to the stage and took the microphone and said, "Please, audience, could we all sit down quietly and enjoy this beautiful wedding, thank you." The hall went quiet and the Reverend took the microphone and thanked Jimmy for making the audience keep quiet. The wedding continued as usual – Kate and Jackson were joined together and became husband and wife.

After pronouncing them husband and wife, the Reverend started to give a short sermon telling the couple what marriage was about and how they need to be a role model for the young ones coming behind. When he wanted to finish his speech, he made a joke of what Robert, Jimmy and Vivian did to Jackson and Kate. The audience laughed for some seconds and he continued his speech. After finishing the speech he used the opportunity to thank the guests and they all stood for a closing hymn.

Jackson and Kate were driven to Kate's hotel to change for the reception party by the wedding organiser. Meanwhile, Kate and Jackson had decided not to go to their honeymoon because of Kate's condition. They fixed their honeymoon for three months after Kate delivered their baby.

After the wedding, Kate and Jackson called the agent that organised the wedding and thanked them very much. Jackson also called some of the guests invited to thank them, despite the letter of appreciation sent to all the guests. Robert, Jimmy and Vivian visited Kate and Jackson at home and they thanked them very much.

Two months after the wedding Kate and Jackson were watching their wedding video in the living room, when Kate started to see water. Jackson called an ambulance, while Kate was rushed to the hospital, where she delivered her baby.